There was the door. I turned the brass knob slowly. Once again I saw the room ablaze with candlelight reflected in the amber ceiling. I turned my eyes to the bed and saw that it was empty. There was no one in the room.

Returning to the corridor, I closed the door behind and felt the soft darkness descend. The creaking I had heard before seemed now to be the sound of footsteps. I glanced behind me and seemed to see a shadow moving!

Terror clutched me and I began to run, not in the direction of my room for that was where the shadow was, but toward the front stairs. I opened my mouth to scream and at the same moment felt something strike my head. There was an explosion of agonizing pain and then...nothing...

A HERITAGE OF STRANGERS

Pamela D'Arcy

A BERKLEY MEDALLION BOOK
published by
BERKLEY PUBLISHING CORPORATION

BERKLEY MEDALLION BOOKS are published by
Berkley Publishing Corporation
200 Madison Avenue
New York, N. Y. 10016

BERKLEY MEDALLION BOOK ® TM 757,375

Printed in the United States of America

Berkley Medallion Edition, MARCH, 1978

A HERITAGE OF STRANGERS

Chapter One

WHEN I AWOKE I knew at once that something was different. Lying quite still with my eyes closed, I heard Nelly bustling about the room. Coals clattered in the grate as she lit the fire. The curtains rustled as she drew them back. She brought the tray to the table by my bed and the tea things rattled. But there was no sound of carriages in the street below. Yes, that was the difference. I caught my breath. Sometime in the early hours of the morning, workmen must have spread straw to muffle the traffic sounds. And I knew all too well what that meant.

Pushing myself up against the bolster, I cried out: "Is he dead? Oh, Nelly, you promised that you'd wake me if there was a turn for the worse."

1

She bent over me, her familiar face soft with sympathy.

"He's still alive, dear, but he's sinking. That's what the doctor says. And you're to go to him as soon as you're dressed. He asked to see you not five minutes ago."

He was conscious then. In spite of the gravity of the situation, I felt a sense of relief. I had been so afraid that he would somehow slip away from me without a word.

Nelly had been my nurse when I was little and she knew my ways. She made no attempt to coax me to drink my tea. A stout figure in black with a shawl about her shoulders, she hurried to the great mahogany cabinet in which my clothes were kept. Within a few minutes I was neatly dressed in my second-best silk and she was skillfully fashioning my long, auburn hair into a bun at the nape of my neck.

"There's always the chance he may rally, whatever the doctor thinks," were her final words as I hurried down the corridor to my father's room.

I was grateful to Nelly for trying to encourage me, but I knew, as soon as I saw his thin, bearded face that there was no hope. His eyes were open, but he seemed to see me from a distance, as though a part of him was no longer in the room.

The nurse hovered about us, a sharp-faced woman, intent on smoothing coverlets and turning pillows. During the first weeks of his illness, my father had often laughed at her when she was out of hearing.

"I believe the poor woman thinks that if I can be kept tidy enough, I'll recover," he had said. "You don't know the tortures I endure at her hands, my dear Ruth. She seems always to have a sponge in her hand. Perpetual cleanliness is her motto. If I as much as rumple the sheets, she's in obvious anguish."

We had laughed then, and tears stung my eyes now
as I realized that we would never laugh again. The good
times—and they had been so good—were over. I shook
my head at the nurse and motioned her away. Before
retreating to her chair in the corner, she murmured
something about the doctor being downstairs having
his breakfast, but I scarcely listened.

"Ruth."

My father's voice was faint. A whisper. I drew a
chair close to the bed and laid my cheek against his.

"Are you in pain?" I asked him.

He was just able to shake his head, but whether to
indicate that he was not or that it did not matter I did
not know. Since the doctor had been giving him
morphine, perhaps he was not in much discomfort. I
ran one hand lightly over the lank, grizzled hair, the
thin cheeks. His skin was cold and damp.

"So young," he whispered. "So young to be left
alone."

The time had passed for reassurances. We had
always been honest with one another and now, when
we both knew that he was about to die, there was no
time for pretense.

"I will have Nelly," I said.

"And a fortune."

For a moment I seemed to see that old glint of
humor in his eyes.

"Never underestimate wealth, my dear," he had told
me once. "Whatever anyone may tell you, it can buy a
good deal of happiness."

I wondered whether I would ever be happy again. I
wanted to bury my head on his chest and weep as I had
so often done when I was a child.

"Cry," he whispered as though he had read my
mind. "Cry if you like, my child."

And so I did. Silently. But without making any

effort to wipe away my tears. Why should he not see me grieve for him? When he was gone, what use would tears be?

"Why?" I said. "Why must it be like this?"

"Some things have no answers."

He smiled faintly. My mentor still. The smile recalled the many happy hours spent together over books. An antiquarian, he had dismissed my governess when he had discovered that I shared his interests.

"It may not be the fashion for women to be intellectuals," he had told me wryly. "And it may be that you will have to hide your abilities when it is time to find a husband. But while you are mine, Ruth, there will be no attempt to deny you knowledge simply because you are not a boy. You are both son and daughter to me, my dear."

"I feel..." I began now.

"As though something important should be said?" The smile was still on his lips.

Nelly had told me that he might rally. But I was not deceived by his brave show. The doctor had said that he was sinking, and I believed him. Even in that smile, there was something unworldly. Often, before death, there was that sudden apparent renewal. This was that moment. And it was as he said. Something important should be spoken between us.

"I love you."

I could think of nothing else to say, and yet it seemed so inadequate. For twenty years this man had been my life. And now he was leaving me. It was all very well for me to say that I had Nelly. But he must know as well as I that without him my world would be a void.

"I want..."

His voice was so faint. I bent my ear close to his lips.

"I want you to be happy."

I tried to smile.

"You are so young..."

It was like listening to a fading echo. I heard the nurse rise and leave the room. No doubt, like me, she sensed that these were the final moments and had gone to fetch the doctor. I was glad that we were alone.

"Your mother..."

I felt myself grow cold. Why, in these final moments, must he speak of her?

His dark eyes focused on mine. I sensed a sudden urgency, as though he had only just realized that time had begun to run away with us.

"You must go to her," he whispered, and his hand crept to cover mine. Bones on flesh.

I wanted to protest. Why should I go to a woman who had abandoned me sixteen years ago? She was a stranger. And why should it be otherwise?

"Part of you... hers," my father said in a voice which was suddenly loud and clear. He struggled to raise himself on the pillows.

"Yes," I said, for in these last minutes he must have sensed protest on my part. And yet I dreaded the commitment I was making. For it was a commitment. Whatever charge he made now, I had to accept it. For so many years I had trusted him. And I had to trust him more than ever in these last moments.

"Promise... promise you will go to her."

"Only tell me why."

The question came reckless to my lips. He had always insisted on questions. He had told me over and over again that the answers are not as important as the questions.

"Because you are... a part of her. Your heritage..."

"Your heritage is the only one I want."

"Promise me."

Dying had made him arbitrary. Never before had he asked me to promise him anything.

"I promise."

The words seemed to release him. Sighing, he sank back on his pillows. Again that smile. But he was a stranger now. I realized that even before his death, he had managed to escape me. Because I did not understand.

"But why?" I asked.

It was the last question, and he could not answer it. I could see that he wanted to. His eyes told me that. But only for a moment. And then they turned to glass. Alive in one moment. Dead in the next.

My head swam. I felt as though I must somehow go after him. But he had slipped behind a corner that I could not find.

When the nurse and the doctor came into the room, I was closing his eyes. The lightest touch of the finger to withered lids.

It was over.

And what remained behind?

Only myself and a promise. A promise I dreaded to keep.

The directions for the funeral were in my father's desk and, as I had guessed, he wanted none of the elaborate display which had lately been encouraged by Queen Victoria's extravagant mourning for her dead consort. "No black plumed horses, no mutes following the carriage, no mad display of flowers." As I read the words, I could hear the ironic twist of his voice.

Thus it was a simple ceremony performed by an Anglican priest at the graveside. The afternoon was foggy and the elaborate Highgate monuments reared their heads like granite beasts around us as we listened to the familiar words of the burial service.

"Dust to dust. Ashes to ashes."

And then it was over. Twelve scholarly gentlemen who had been my father's closest friends returned with

Nelly and me to the house in Sloan Square and stayed for an hour, sipping sherry and eating the small cakes which Cook had insisted on preparing. Each gentleman in turn offered his condolences. The proprieties were observed.

It was the sort of sober, unemotional gathering of which my father would have approved, and for that I was glad. What female friends I had had sent messages of sympathy, but I had invited none of them to attend the funeral since they had not known my father well. His memory was kept fresher with only his friends gathered, as they had been so many times before in this same drawing room.

It was with relief, however, that I saw them to the door. Only one more ordeal remained, and that was to listen to the reading of the will, which Mr. Harlow, my father's solicitor, performed with dispatch in the library.

"Everything was left to you, my dear," he told me, settling his spectacles on his nose and beaming at me in his usual jovial fashion. "This house and a substantial fortune safely invested in consols. I—er, understand that your father completely informed you as to the details of those investments."

"Yes," I said, wearily. "I will want to go over them with you at an early opportunity. And, of course, there is the matter of the house in Oxfordshire."

It was an awkward subject, but one which I knew must be discussed. I knew very little about Ludden Hall except that it had been in my father's family for three generations and that after separating from my father sixteen years before, it had been my mother's residence.

"Your mother realizes that she is free to remain there until my death," my father had told me in the early days of his illness. "After that, you must make the decision as to whether she remains. I have stipulated that you must remain the owner. The house cannot be sold. Other than that, the choice of whether or not she continues to live there is yours. I made an adequate settlement on her many years ago and she is financially independent. There is no need for you to feel that you have any obligation, moral or otherwise, to provide for her."

It was the only time I could recall that he had spoken to me of her. I suppose that when she had left us so many years ago, he must have discussed the matter with me. But since I had been only four at the time, I could not remember what he had said. Any further information concerning my mother had come from Nelly who had said little, but enough to indicate that I would do well to forget her and that my father was not to be bothered by questions.

Of course I had been curious. But I was forced into the position of providing my own answers. My friends had mothers who lavished affection on them. Since I had none, it had to be that she did not love me. Certainly she could not love my father or she would never have left him. As I grew older I realized that the separation might well have been the result of a mutual decision—one not taken lightly since a broken family was frowned on by society, despite the fact that a divorce law had recently been passed.

I knew that my mother had been notified of my father's death for Mr. Harlow had told me at the time that he would do so. When I had suggested that it might be more appropriate for me to inform her myself, he had frowned and advised me that he thought my father would have preferred that the letter come from him. I told him then, of course, that my father had expressed a desire that I see her.

"I doubt that your mother will come to London for the funeral," Mr. Harlow had replied, jingling his watch chain nervously. "She had become, I believe, something of a recluse. But, of course, she may write to you."

"She has never written before," I told him, trying to keep the bitterness from my voice.

"Yes. Well, at all events, it is my advice that you take no steps in the matter of communicating with her until the will is read."

And with that the subject was dropped and I was too wrapped up in my grief to give it another thought. But now, obviously, I had to deal with it.

"As far as I am concerned," I said slowly, "my mother can remain at Ludden Hall as long as she cares to."

"Yes, yes. Quite so. But things are not necessarily that simple, I'm afraid. You have already told me that your father wished you to see her. And there are certain provisions in the will concerning that—er, meeting. Perhaps you would like to have me read . . ."

"It will be simpler if you tell me what is to be done," I assured him.

"Very well. There is a letter here, written by your father and addressed to your mother. It was his wish that you deliver it to her in person, along with this case, the contents of which you are to inspect now in my presence."

I had not noticed the case until Mr. Harlow pushed it toward me. Covered with scarlet plush, it was the size of a large Bible. After inserting a small gold key in its lock, the soliciter pulled back the cover, disclosing a jumble of jewelry resting on the red, satin lining.

It was an amazing collection of necklaces, bracelets and brooches, all in the worst possible taste. Not bothering to hide my amazement, I picked up each piece in turn and examined it carefully.

There was a necklace ringed with scarlet coral cameos set in silver, and another of jet with white porcelain centers, while a third sported Scottish pebbles set in gold. A soapstone brooch inlaid with turquoise flowers had become attached to a gold bracelet in the Etruscan style faced with a broad glass chamber in which a lock of faded blond hair was displayed. An art nouveau bracelet shaped like a serpent followed. There were rings, as well, one featuring the head of the late Prince Albert. Various pieces featured seed pearls.

"There is an inventory," Mr. Harlow assured me as I piled the lot back into the case. "The value is not great. A curious collection, is it not?"

Curious was scarcely the word. My father's taste in jewelry, as in all things, had been faultless. Thinking of the rope of perfectly matched pearls he had given me, and looking down at my emerald ring set in an eighteenth-century setting, I could not believe that the man who had chosen such pieces with loving care would ever have purchased these horrors.

"You say the will directs me to take this—this collection to my mother?"

Mr. Harlow nodded solemnly. "He gave me the case some sixteen years ago to put in safe-keeping. I seem to recall his saying that he did not want it in the house."

Sixteen years ago—the year he and my mother had separated.

"But he would never have purchased this sort of thing," I protested. "And if they are my mother's, then how does it happen that she did not take them with her when she left?"

Mr. Harlow shook his bald head. "I wish I could provide you with answers, my dear, but it is as much a mystery to me as it is to you."

A knock came on the door and Sally, the upstairs maid, entered with a tray laden with tea things. Cook, convinced as always that only the frequent consumption of the powerful liquid she brewed would keep up my spirits, had asserted herself.

I could have done without the distraction, but Mr.

Harlow watched me pour with distinct approval and took the opportunity to speak of my future.

"Have you had time to make plans, my child?" he asked me with his usual benevolence.

Such a question from a slight acquaintance would have been an impertinence, perhaps, but I had known this rotund gentleman since I was a child and I smiled at him.

"Would it shock you if I said that I am thinking of taking a position as a cataloguer at the British Museum?"

"A position, Miss Bramwell! There is no need, I assure you. Perhaps I have not made myself clear. You have been left a very wealthy young woman."

"My father would have approved of my doing something," I told him. "After all, I acted as his assistant for several years. And I have no desire, you know, to fill my life with afternoon calls."

He nodded, but I could see from his bespectacled eyes that he did not really understand.

"As you know," I went on, "I have a certain knowledge of antiques and nothing would suit me better than to work at such a fine museum. Dr. Galloway who, as I'm sure you know, is an expert in Byzantine mosaics, has offered me an appointment. My father and he were close friends."

"But a paying position. . . ."

"I would take it without pay," I told him. "I need to feel that in some small way I am carrying on my father's work."

"Indeed!" the solicitor blustered, removing his spectacles and wiping them furiously with a silk handkerchief. "I must confess, my dear, that you have taken me by surprise. You are a beautiful young woman. Surely you must intend to marry."

"Perhaps," I said, "but at the moment the idea has little attraction."

"But such a waste. I mean to say, to think of you

buried in a museum.... I must say I have long thought that your father kept you much too engaged in pursuits which properly belong to men. I realize that you may feel that you can best honor his memory by making this gesture, but...."

"I will honor that and myself as well," I assured him. "And now, I think, we must turn ourselves to immediate problems. I have been charged with the delivery of this letter and the jewelry to my mother. Until that is accomplished, I can scarcely think of my future."

"Yes, yes. I suppose that must come first. Perhaps you would like me to write to her, explaining the necessity for such a meeting."

"No," I said. "I will write myself. Today."

I paused and then went on quickly. "Tell me, did you know her?"

Again Mr. Harlow removed his spectacles and this time made a great business indeed of polishing them.

"Why yes, my dear," he said finally. "I had the pleasure of meeting the lady."

"I think," I said carefully, "that if I must see her, it would help me to know something of what to expect. Please do not misunderstand me. I have no interest in the cause of her separation from my father. I simply want to know what sort of woman I am to deal with."

Little beads of perspiration appeared on Mr. Harlow's forehead. "Well, of course it was a long time ago," he said, "but I remember her as being very beautiful. Like yourself, my dear. The same auburn hair and oval face. High cheekbones. Yes, quite charming."

"I did not mean her appearance," I said evenly. "What sort of woman is she?"

He seemed to brace himself.

"As for what she is now, I cannot tell. But when she still lived here at Sloan Square she was—well, a rather impetuous woman. Given, I fear, to a certain arrogance of manner. Her father was a peer of the realm, as no doubt you know."

I shook my head. "I know nothing of that side of the family, if one is to call it that."

"Lord Ramsdale was a—well, a bit of an eccentric who lost his fortune at the gaming table."

"But my mother? We were speaking of my mother."

"I don't know what else I can tell you," he said, shuffling papers. "She did not appear to be an intellectual, but she had—a certain force of character."

I saw that there was little else to be pried from him.

"And of course," he reminded me as I rose from my chair, "there is no telling what she has become. I can only warn you..."

"Yes," I said, suddenly intent.

"Perhaps your meeting with her should be brief. An afternoon call. There is no need for you to stay at Ludden Hall. I can recommend an excellent inn at Oxford...."

He broke off in confusion.

"Is there any particular reason why I should not stay with her?" I pressed him.

"No, indeed. None that I know of. I will say no more on the subject."

I accompanied him to the door and there he pressed my hand.

"Be cautious, my child," he said. "You have not been much exposed to the real world and many strange things happen there. Yes, many strange things, indeed. I would not see you hurt."

Five days later a letter arrived from Oxfordshire. If my letter to my mother had been brief, hers was abrupt.

"Come if you like," she wrote. "Ludden Hall is yours. I can scarcely keep you away."

Not one word about my father. Not even a touch of

graciousness. Mr. Harlow had called her imperious.
Now I knew her to be lacking in all sensibility as well.
Crumpling the letter in a ball and throwing it in the
fireplace, I realized that, although I had not admitted it
to myself, I had hoped to receive a response which
would prove she had some feeling for me.

My first reaction when my anger had cooled was not
to go. Surely if my father had known that she would
insult me in such a way, he would not have sent me to
Ludden Hall. Then, as reason reasserted itself, I
reflected that he might have known all too well how she
would respond to my advances. Perhaps, I told myself,
he had wanted to be sure that I entertained no
delusions about my mother. Once he was dead, I might
well have found myself drawn into a fanciful world in
which I dreamed that my one remaining parent loved
me. Yes, of course. Over a period of time, I might have
succumbed to hopes which later would have been
shattered. Better, he might well have reasoned, that I
should see the woman for what she was as soon as
possible.

If that was the bitter medicine he wished me to
swallow, then I would swallow it at once. But quickly. I
determined to take Nelly with me to Oxford where I
would book rooms at an inn and send a message to
Ludden Hall announcing my arrival.

Once I started to make specific plans, I found myself
feeling much better. I would go to my mother the next
morning after my arrival in Oxford, not as a
sentimental child, but as a woman carrying out a
distasteful commission. I would hand her the letter and
the jewelry case and leave directly. That was, after all,
only what was necessary to carry out my charge. And I
would make it quite clear to her that I had only come
because my father wished it and for no other reason. I
would match her indifference with my own.

Going to the gilt vanity table, I stared at my flushed

face in the mirror. Mr. Harlow had said that I looked like her. At the time the idea had displeased me, but now I was glad. I would punish her with my own youth. I would wear my finest black silk and, since the autumn days were turning cold, my fur-lined cape. Yes, and the fine cameo my father had given me, a delicately carved ornament which would put the tawdry jewelry I was delivering to her to shame. I was wealthy. I had taste and intellect. And, because I owned the very house in which she lived, I had power.

I gave myself up to wild daydreams. Perhaps I would contact the estate agent—for there must be such a person to manage the property—and give him certain directives about the maintenance of Ludden Hall. Perhaps there were certain repairs I could order. Workmen about the place would serve as an ample reminder to her that I had assumed the rights of ownership. At the very least, they would remind her of her position.

I had never felt vindictive before and the strength of that unfamiliar emotion frightened me. All my suppressed feelings toward a mother who had left me were suddenly crystalized into hatred. Seeking to calm myself, I opened the jewelry case Mr. Harlow had left with me, and began to sort through its contents. I checked each piece against the inventory which had apparently been made out at the time my father had left the case with his solicitor, since his signature and that of Mr. Harlow were on the sheet, followed by a date— June 30, 1854.

Sixteen years ago. I would never know what had happened then to drive apart two people who had presumably loved one another. I reminded myself that I did not care.

I was holding the serpent bracelet in my hand when Nelly came into the room. Turning, I saw a look of horror on her face.

"Where did you get that, Miss Ruth?" she demanded, her plump face sinking in on itself.

I explained as concisely as I could.

"This and the other pieces of jewelry in this case are to be delivered by me to my mother at Ludden Hall," I added. "It was my father's wish."

She stood beside me, staring down into the case as though it were a coffin. Her usually ruddy face was pale, and her breath came unevenly.

"The master never could have wanted you to do such a thing," she whispered.

"One of the last things he said to me was that I must see my mother," I told her, curious at the violence of her response. "There is no mistake. I have had a letter from her this morning, bidding me to come if I like. We will leave tomorrow."

"We, Miss?"

"I want you to accompany me, Nelly."

"I could never stay in the same house with her!" she said in a shrill voice. "Don't ask it of me, Miss Ruth."

"Neither of us will stay at Ludden Hall," I told her, "although it is mine now and my mother only stays there with my consent. We will take rooms at an inn in Oxford and return to London the next day as soon as I have delivered these things and a letter to her."

"A letter?" From the frightened look on Nelly's face, I might have announced that I intended to deliver guns to a British outpost in India.

"Written by my father," I told her. "I have no knowledge of its contents. Perhaps he had some last message for her. It is not my affair. I am to deliver it. Nothing more."

"I beg you not to go, Miss."

As though her legs would no longer hold her, Nelly sank down on the bed and buried her face in her wrinkled hands.

"Tell me why you are so concerned," I said softly,

but with a note of command in my voice.

"She is an evil woman."

Lifting her hands, Nelly stared at me intently as though begging me to believe her.

A thin shock of anxiety struck me. Nelly was a practical person, not given to flights of imagination. To her things were good or bad, improper or proper, dirty or clean. I had never heard the word "evil" on her lips before.

"You must tell me what you mean," I said slowly. "My mother's letter told me that she is an unpleasant woman. Mr. Harlow says that she is imperious. Arrogant. But evil? That is another matter, and I think you must explain."

It was obvious that Nelly was making an attempt to gain control of herself. Rising, she folded her hands primly in front of her.

"I did not mean to say it," she told me.

"Ah, but say it you did," I replied, letting the serpent bracelet slide onto my arm.

With a swiftness I would not have guessed possible, Nelly bent forward and pulled it from my wrist.

I had told myself that I wanted to know nothing of the past. And that was true. But I loved this woman and had since childhood. I could not let her act in such a strange way and not know why.

"These *are* my mother's jewels, then," I said. "You hated her—or feared her.... Yes, I think you feared her and you cannot bear to see me wearing anything that was hers. Is that true?"

Nelly bowed her head.

I took the bracelet from her, flung it in the case and closed the scarlet plush cover.

"I would not give you pain for anything," I said gently. "But you must tell me this. Did my father give her these—these things?"

She raised her head and I saw that her face was

troubled. Indeed she looked as though she would soon break into tears.

"A simple yes or no, Nelly."

"No, Miss Ruth. How could he have bought such trinkets? You know..."

"But they were hers?"

"Yes, Miss."

"You are not usually this reticent with me, Nelly."

"The sight of those—those things took me back. I remembered how fond she was of them. Many's the time I saw her taking them out of that case and running her fingers over them."

She grimaced and it came to me that my mother must have been an awesome woman indeed to have inspired such a response in a woman like Nelly sixteen years after she and this house had seen the last of her.

"I will not trouble you with any other questions, but this," I said softly. "If my father did not buy the serpent bracelet and the rest, then did my mother buy them for herself?"

Again that look of fear blurred the pale blue eyes.

"I—I do not know. I swear it!"

She was lying. I knew her too well to think otherwise. And I had never heard her lie before.

"Is it possible," I said, "that another man beside my father gave her these jewels as gifts?"

I spoke the thought as soon as it came to my mind and was aware of a sense of exhilaration. Perhaps I had stumbled onto the cause of my parents' separation. Some man. A lover. Someone lacking in as much taste as she. Perhaps my father had kept the jewels as a reminder—or as a threat. Women could be divorced if adultery could be proved against them. With men it was a different matter. Under the law they need pay no price for infidelity. But a woman could be ruined.

"Tell me, Nelly," I persisted.

"I do not know."

There was a note of stubbornness in her voice which I knew not to challenge.

"Then there is nothing more to be said on the subject," I sighed. "Very well. Let us begin to pack my things. Remember that I will want my best black silk and the fur cape."

Chapter Two

THE MITRE WAS a comfortable old inn on a quiet
sidestreet of Oxford with colleges on three sides of it
and shops on the other. I had not needed Mr. Harlow
to recommend the place. It was where my father had
always stayed when he had visited his old friends at
Magdalen College, from which he had taken his degree
and where he had taught before he married. As it
happened my father had never brought me with him on
these visits, saying that I would be bored by the talk of
old scholars. Now, peering out my casement window at
the spires which punctured the sky above this lovely
university town, I wished that I had insisted on sharing
with him this part of his past.

It was then that I thought of Professor Rankin. My father had often spoken of him and I knew that he had been a great friend. I had never met him for he had never seemed to come to London, but he had written a letter of sympathy after my father's death, a moving letter in which he had expressed a hope that we might meet someday.

What better time than now, I mused? As soon as we had unpacked, Nelly had retired to her own room, advising me to rest. But I was in far too high strung a state to do so. There had been the note to write to my mother, telling her that I would call on her at eleven the next morning. After a messenger had been sent with it to Ludden Hall, I had tried to lie down. But I was too restless. The remainder of the afternoon and the evening to come seemed to be interminably long. I had thought of wandering around town, but now it occurred to me that I could better pass my time in the company of Professor Rankin if he were free. He could tell me about the old times when he and my father were young.

Impetuously I scribbled a note inviting him to dine with me at the inn. The boy who carried the message returned almost at once with a gracious request from Professor Rankin that I dine with him at his rooms at Magdalen. It was a heaven sent opportunity to see the college which was so closely associated with my father's past and I accepted with pleasure.

Nelly helped me dress, dour but apparently unable to think of any reason why I should not go. But she insisted on accompanying me to the gates of the college, apparently under the apprehension that a town so full of undergraduates presented untold dangers to a young woman walking alone.

It was a lovely evening with the setting sun mellowing the stone walls of the colleges which we passed. We made our way down the High where carriages rattled up and down over the cobblestones and scholars hurried past, black gowns fluttering from their shoulders. I found myself wishing that I had been my father's son, for then I would be a student here, one of the company of young men talking eagerly together by college gates.

The street led down to the river which flowed tranquil under the arched stone bridge. For a moment I paused to watch the young men punting below, and then looked up at the graceful tower of the college chapel which my father had so often described to me. Dismissing Nelly, I made my way to the porter's lodge. A tall, silver-haired gentleman wearing evening dress was standing there.

"My dear Ruth," he said, stretching out his hands.

Although he tried to disguise the fact, I could see that the sight of me had disconcerted him. And yet he was expecting me. Perhaps, although he did not say so, it was because I looked, as Mr. Harlow had said, so like my mother.

But her name was not mentioned. As we descended the stairs to the cloisters where a covered walk edged a rectangular garden, Professor Rankin spoke softly of the sorrow with which he had received word of my father's death.

"I am so glad that you let me know you were here," he told me as we mounted the stairs at the north corner of the cloisters and emerged into an open country setting, edged with tall stone buildings and a deer park where, in the evening shadows, those graceful creatures grazed. The town seemed to be far away and I caught my breath at the beauty of it all. How could my father ever have left this lovely place, I wondered? Had my mother insisted? Could it be that, daughter of a peer, she had considered the role of wife of a university don beneath her?

But I had promised not to ask myself such

questions. I only wanted to know something of the man my father had been before he had met her, and this picture was one Professor Rankin was willing enough to sketch for me. Over dinner, which was expertly served by his man in a comfortable sitting room where gaslight discreetly illuminated the fine paintings on the walls and glass-fronted cases full of books, he talked easily and well of a time nearly fifty years ago when he and my father had been undergraduates together.

Sipping wine from a long stemmed goblet with the flickering light of the fire glinting the elegant silver and plate, I found myself relaxing.

"We had rooms on the same floor," the professor told me. "It wasn't long before we were the closest of friends. And we were a bit wild for the first two years, although I suppose you find that difficult to believe, looking at me now. But there was a time when sitting up all night with a decanter of good port and the company of friends seemed more important than the lectures we were bound to miss the next day. We were both very fond of boating, too, and your father made varsity. And then there were the nights on the town. Many the time we bribed the porter to let us in, or if old Jackson was on duty, we climbed the walls. That was a bit of a feat then, as it is now, since the top was studded with jagged glass. But that only made it more of an adventure."

There was no end to his reminiscences, and I listened eagerly to stories of papers left unwritten and angry tutors. During the long holidays they had taken walking tours, sometimes to Devon and other times to Scotland.

"My family home was in Somerset and your father came there with me as often as though he were my brother. As you know, your father's own parents were dead by then."

I did not interrupt him to say that I knew nothing

about when my grandparents had died or under what conditions. And yet the realization that I had not known was painful. Why, I wondered, had I never asked questions? Was it because in some subtle way my father had raised me to believe that the past, as far as it concerned his own life, was unimportant?

Professor Rankin was talking about his own father now.

"He was indulgent with me," he said, "and, of course, your father had an ample allowance administered by the executor of the estate—a London solicitor, I believe. If we had kept on with folly until your father was twenty-one, I might have helped him to squander the fortune that came to him then. But by that time we had settled down to serious scholarship. Both of us earned firsts in Classics. But, of course, you know all this."

I shook my head.

"My father described the college to me, and he often spoke of you, but he never went into detail about the past. It was as though it were painful for him to think of it, as though something had been lost... I mean, I believe he loved his life here so much that it hurt him to remember."

"Yes," Professor Rankin said in a low voice. "I think perhaps it did. He rarely returned to Oxford after...."

"After his marriage?"

"Yes. Even after your mother was—no longer with him in London. Perhaps the proximity of Ludden Hall...."

He paused as though uncertain as to whether or not he should go on.

I did not want our conversation to end this way.

"You said that my father often went home with you," I murmured. "Tell me, did he never go to Ludden Hall as a young man? After all, as you say, it is nearby and it was his family home. He had no other."

"I think the place aroused too many unhappy memories," the professor said. "Perhaps it simply lost all meaning to him when his parents died. And then, of course, his older brother died tragically."

I nodded, glad that this news, at least, did not come as a surprise to me. My father had mentioned his brother once, although I realized now he had never spoken his name. But I knew that one holiday when my father was about seventeen and in his last year at Eton, his brother had drowned in a river on the family estate. He had said no more than that about it, but it had been clear to me that even after so many years, the memory was painful to him.

"You *do* know about your uncle then," Professor Rankin said, sounding strangely relieved. "I'm sure that all of the circumstances combined to make your father uncomfortable at Ludden Hall, although he visited it from time to time. More often than not, I went with him. I think he only visited the place to assure himself that it was being kept up. There were always servants there, but I don't think I ever saw the furniture without dust sheets over it. We never stayed the night. I often thought that strange, but I never pressed him. What he told me was said voluntarily."

There was a pause. The fire hissed in the grate.

"I am going to Ludden Hall tomorrow," I said in a low voice. "At my father's express wish."

Professor Rankin did no more than incline his head, but the look in his eyes encouraged me to go on. Not until this moment had I realized how badly I needed to talk to someone about the duty which now loomed so near. I had asked my father why I must go, but he had died before he could answer. And apparently Mr. Harlow knew no more about the matter than I did. But this man was different. It was just possible that he could explain why my father had wanted me to visit the house he had spent a lifetime avoiding. I realized suddenly that, in spite of my brave intentions for the morrow, I badly needed a rationale for what I was about to do.

But I could not embarrass the professor with a direct request. Instead I simply stated my charge, adding only that I had not seen my mother since childhood and that her single communication with me during the past week had been something less than gracious.

Professor Rankin shook his head sorrowfully.

"I guessed something of the enmity between your mother and father," he said slowly, "although, mind you, he never spoke of the reason for their separation. Perhaps he thought that with him gone, you might need her. But I realize how difficult it will be for you to go to Ludden Hall, my dear. I only wish that I could give you some advice."

I swallowed my disappointment. He could not help me then. Unless. . . .

"Did you ever meet her?" I asked him.

His pale blue eyes met mine directly and there was none of the reluctance in his response which Mr. Harlow and Nelly had shown.

"Your father had been a don here at Magdalen for ten years when he met your mother," he said. "As it happened I was with him at the time. Her father, Lord Ramsdale, had taken a house near Abingdon where he often entertained members of the college. Perhaps, having fallen on hard times, he liked to surround himself with young university men to remind himself of better days. He had lost his Dorset estate by then and, although he lived well, it was in rented houses."

He smiled ruefully. "Lord Ramsdale was a strange man," he said. "Very much the eccentric. But even though he was in debt to everyone by the time I met him, I have never known a man to set a better table. And he collected interesting people. Artists. Writers."

I looked at him, puzzled, for he seemed to be speaking of a different man than the one Mr. Harlow had described simply as a gambler.

"Mad about the turf, of course," Professor Rankin went on. "He spent a good deal of his time at Newmarket, I believe. But your father and I knew him as a host. He amused us. Provided stimulating company. And, of course, there was his daughter. Young. Beautiful. You're the very picture of her with that mass of auburn hair. The resemblance startled me when I first saw you this evening. Really, it's quite extraordinary. And then there was the romantic appeal of her widowhood. Such a young woman. Your father was not the only one who was impressed, I assure you."

"A widow!" I gasped. "You mean she had been married before?"

The professor leaned back in his chair.

"Of course I thought you knew," he said apologetically. "Forgive me if I have been indiscreet."

"But I want to know," I told him with some urgency. What a fool I had been to pretend to myself that I wanted to know nothing about the woman who was my mother.

"Ah, but I will never forgive myself for having made such an error," the silver-haired gentleman said, shaking his head slowly.

"I would have found out in time," I told him. "Besides, it scarcely matters."

"That is not what I mean, my dear. If I had realized how little your father had told you, I would never have invited David to come here tonight."

"David?"

"David Warrendon," Professor Rankin replied reluctantly. "He is a fellow here. When I met him in the quadrangle this afternoon soon after receiving your message, I mentioned that you were dining with me. And, since he seemed so eager to meet you again. . . ."

"But who is David Warrendon?" I demanded.

"Your mother's stepson by her first marriage," the professor said abruptly. "I never dreamed that you had no knowledge of his existence. Perhaps there's still time to put him off. I can send a note to his rooms."

But even as he rose and started toward the rosewood desk in the corner, a knock sounded on the door.

Professor Rankin rose and looked down at me questioningly.

"I realize what a great shock this must have been for you," he said quietly. "I blame David for not explaining the—the circumstances. Perhaps it would be best if I offered some excuse and sent him away. A meeting between you might be most awkward, particularly at this time."

"No!" I protested. "I—I confess to being disconcerted, to discover that I have a stepbrother. But no. I want to meet him."

Apparently the professor's man had opened the door in the adjoining room for I could hear muted conversation. Professor Rankin hurried out and I realized that he was probably determined to speak to David alone before introducing him to me.

Alone, I set to composing myself. When the two men came into the room, I was pretending to examine a calf-bound volume of Tennyson's verse.

"Allow me to present David Warrendon," Professor Rankin said in a low voice.

I looked up, a set smile on my lips. My stepbrother was very tall and slender, but his face was cut in a rugged mold and his eyes were dark brown.

"Professor Rankin has explained," he said simply. "And I must apologize for intruding in this way. I had no idea that you would not remember me. Of course you were very young when we last saw one another, but. . . ."

"We have met before?"

I let the book fall to my lap to disguise the fact that my hands were shaking.

"I was eight when your father married my stepmother," David said. "Already in boarding school. But I came to the house in Sloan Square for the holidays."

"I'm sorry," I told him. "I don't remember."

In silence we looked at one another. Professor Rankin's man was deftly clearing the table and the professor himself was busy pulling chairs close to the fire, but these activities took place on the periphery of my consciousness.

"Perhaps," I heard our host say, "you would like to be alone together."

"No," David and I said at once.

"Then we will sit and talk," the professor said. "Here, David. Take this chair next to your—next to Ruth. Will you have a glass of port?"

"Thank you."

Without taking his eyes from me, my stepbrother sat down, a handsome figure in evening dress. A handsome stranger. There was an awkward silence while the professor went to a side table to fetch a decanter.

"I want to remember," I said to the young man beside me, surprised at my own audactiy. "Please help me."

David seemed to understand.

"When I was twelve and you were three, we spent August at St. Ives in Devon," he said slowly. "Every morning your nurse took you to the beach and I came too and built sand castles which you took a certain delight in destroying."

He smiled. "You were a delightful child," he said. "But impetuous. You made me laugh, but your nurse took a dim view of such behavior and made you apologize to me. And apologize you always would in a perfectly charming manner. Then when the next castle was built, you would knock it down again."

For a moment I felt myself on the verge of remembering. Waves. Hot sand under my hands. And then—nothing.

"I'm sorry," I said again.

My voice was even, but inside I was engulfed with sudden anger. Nelly had been my nurse on that long-ago trip to St. Ives. She had known David. But she had never mentioned him to me. Why? There could only be one answer. My father must have ordered it. But for what possible reason? Because he wanted to sever all my emotional ties with my mother and everyone related to her? But why? David and I were not related by blood. We had neither the same mother nor father.

As though he had read my mind, David said:

"How strange that you were never so much as reminded of my existence. I was twelve when my mother moved to Ludden Hall. She explained to me, of course, that she and your father were to be permanently estranged, although she has never to this day told me why. Your father and I were never particularly close, although I respected him. But I was very fond of you— as though you were my real sister—and I was insistent about seeing you again."

He sipped his port and set the goblet down carefully on the marble-topped table beside him. The professor sat silent, watching us. Not intruding. I wondered if any of this made any sense to him. He had known my father as neither David nor I had. Perhaps, later, he could offer some explanation.

"My mother told me that the arrangements for the separation included the provision that she would never see you again," David continued. "Until you were a woman, that is, and then it would be your choice. I was amazed, naturally. I asked questions. But there were never any answers. And when I asked to be allowed to go to London to visit you, there was a flat refusal. Something about my mother's face frightened me. I never asked again."

My anger fled. Now I was afraid. I felt as though a great void had opened in front of me and that I had no choice but to step into it, no matter what the danger.

"You said that it had been arranged that my mother would never see me again while I was a child," I said in a voice which seemed strangely unlike my own.

"That was what I was told," David said.

"Don't you see what this means?" I demanded. "I grew up believing that she had abandoned me. Voluntarily. But you—you're implying that my father made the decision. That he arbitrarily decided that if my mother wished to leave him, she had to leave me as well."

I could feel the tears welling up in my eyes. Despising myself for a show of weakness, I dashed them away with the back of my hand.

"I can't believe that of him," I went on. "My father was a kind man. A loving man. He would never have been so cruel as to keep me from my own mother, no matter what happened between them."

The professor had risen and was hovering about me, holding a glass of port.

"Here, my dear," he said. "Drink just a bit of this. It will help to steady you."

I shook my head. "No," I said. "I'm quite all right, I assure you. But none of this makes any sense. I was allowed to think I had been abandoned. That my mother didn't want me. My father never said it in so many words, but he must have known what I believed. And when he was dying, he must have realized that I would find out the truth. He sent me here, knowing I would probably meet you, or at least find out that you existed. And yet he never said a word to prepare me."

"If I may be allowed to say one thing," Professor

Rankin murmured, returning to his chair. "Your father never acted without reason, Ruth. You must know that as well as I. Doubtlessly in time it will all be clear and you will see that he had your best interests at heart."

"There is still the fact that you were allowed to grow up believing that your mother—our mother—was a heartless monster," David said in a level voice. Until this moment he had showed no emotion, but now I saw that he was angry.

"She could have proved to me differently," I said quickly. My love for my father was too deeply entrenched to be uprooted all of a sudden. I knew that the time was coming—was, perhaps, already here—when I must see him in a different light. But whatever he had done, I would defend him to the last. It was as Professor Rankin said. He had been a reasonable man, above all. If he had specified, as part of the terms of separation, that my mother never see me while I was still an impressionable child, then he must have had good reason.

"I'm afraid I don't know what you mean," David said in a cool voice.

"She could have come to the funeral," I told him. "At the very least she could have written me. Shown some feeling. Do you know how she responded when I wrote to tell her that I was coming to Ludden Hall? She said that I could come if I liked. Something to that effect. I'm far too upset to remember the exact words. But the point is that my father, in commissioning me to come to her, was opening the door to her. I'm a woman now, not a child. Nothing in their agreement keeps her from showing some affection now. It simply is not possible that he forced her to promise him that she would never show any affection to me, even after he was dead. Whatever agreement was made between them must have terminated when my father died. And yet she told me to come if I liked!"

Leaning forward, David touched my hand. It was
clear from the way he looked at me that he was no
longer angry.

"Our mother is not an ordinary woman," he said
slowly. "This is difficult to explain. But remember, I
was twelve when she left your father. Quite old enough
to see the change in her. She had been—well, high
spirited. She loved to sing, dance. I'm making her
sound frivolous, I know, and perhaps she was. I always
wondered why she made the sort of second marriage
she did. I scarcely remember my own father, but from
what my grandfather tells me, he was as high spirited as
she. Neither of them were intellectuals. And yet, after
he died—it was a hunting accident—my mother chose
to marry. . . ."

"Wait!" I interrupted him. "You spoke of your
grandfather just now as though he were alive."

"But of course he is," David replied. "He lives at
Ludden Hall with my mother. You *were* kept in total
ignorance of that side of the family, weren't you? It's
quite unbelievable."

My eyes sought Professor Rankin. I could see that
he was taken as much by surprise as I.

"When you spoke of Lord Ramsdale earlier," I said
breathlessly, "you spoke of him as though he were
dead."

"I swear that I thought he was," Professor Rankin
said. "Simple assumption, of course. He must be a very
old man by now."

"Ninety-two," David said with a touch of pride in
his voice. "And as independent minded as ever. A
determined eccentric. I think you may like him, Ruth."

My mind whirled. I heard the professor say, "But
you never mentioned him, David."

"If you'll think back, sir, you'll realize that I rarely
speak of my family. What conversations you and I

have had have been of an academic nature. I assure you
that I had no reason to wish to hide my grandfather's
existence."

"But of course I made no such implication,"
Professor Rankin began.

I took a deep breath. "It's growing late," I said. "I
must leave and yet, there seem to be so many things I
don't know."

I paused, remembering those last moments of my
father's life. "Why?" I had asked him at the end. The
questions should never have been delayed until then.
Until now I had believed that had he been given the
time, a reprieve from death, he would have answered
me. But now I wondered.

"I'll find you a cab," David said, rising. "Don't think
me unsympathetic, Ruth. I can see how difficult this
has been for you."

"And there is tomorrow to come," I murmured,
surrendering to a sense of dread. What a fool I had
been to think that the meeting with my mother could be
a brief, insignificant encounter. Perhaps she had been
cold in her response to my attempt to make her feel her
dependency on me. With so many questions to be
answered I could scarcely hand her the letter and the
box of jewels and depart, head held high. I was at her
mercy, not she at mine. Unless she would explain the
past to me, I was fated to live the rest of my life not
knowing what sort of man my father had really been.

And I had been so sure I knew him. So sure.

"I have rooms here at the college," David was
saying. "But if you like, I will go with you to Ludden
Hall tomorrow. It might make the meeting easier."

"No," I told him. "My father intended me to go
alone. And that is the way it must be. No matter how
difficult it is. I—I trusted him. I still trust him. He
charted the course and I owe it to him to follow it."

* * *

"The only reason I insisted that you come to Ludden Hall is that I must know if she has changed."

If Nelly recognized my tone as one of apology, she gave no sign, continuing to look out the window of the carriage as though absorbed by the spectacular view of the spires of Oxford.

The carriage had lumbered up Boar Hill and now the coachman was cracking the whip to turn the horses onto a narrow road lined on one side by a hawthorn hedge and on the other by a high stone wall.

"You don't have to say a word," I went on impatiently. "For heaven sake, Nelly, look at me. Don't make things more difficult than they are already."

"Perhaps you wouldn't be so edgy if you'd had a good night's sleep, Miss," Nelly replied. "Staying out until nearly eleven. . . ."

She did not look as though she had slept well herself. Her plump face was white and there were dark shadows under her eyes as she turned to look at me accusingly. The sun was shining and it was warm for October, but she pulled her black shawl tight about her as though she were chilled.

Probably I had been wrong, I thought, to have told her that I had met David. But she had fussed about me so the night before as she had helped me undress that I had yielded to temptation. She had been turning down the sheets to put the copper warming pan in place when I burst out with the news. It seemed strange, I told her, that she should spend so much time thinking of my physical comfort and give so little thought to my emotional well-being.

"Why didn't you tell me that I had a stepbrother?" I demanded, climbing into the high bed and propping the bolster behind me.

Nelly stared at me incredulously as I went on to explain how David and I had met.

"Did you keep silent about him because of my father?" I asked her insistently. "Did he tell you never to mention David?"

She turned away, but not before I saw the expression on her face. There was no need for her to answer. I knew how loyal she had been to the man who had been her master for twenty years. And I felt a sudden sense of guilt for having put her in such a position.

"Whatever he did, he did for your own good," she said, unconsciously paraphrasing Professor Rankin.

I had not pressed her after that. I was not at all upset, I assured her. Only surprised. Confused. But, yes, I would sleep.

But of course I did not sleep. Dawn was breaking when I finally fell into a restless sort of doze. Shadows of dreams. And then a sudden drop into complete wakefulness with every nerve in my body tingling.

I was nervous still, but determined not to show it. I smoothed the black silk of my gown about my knees with gloved hands and drew the collar of the fur-lined cape high about my neck. I had chosen a deep bonnet which nearly hid my hair. If there was an extraordinary resemblance between my mother and me, I was intent on disguising it in any way that I could.

"Try not to hate her," David had said to me the night before when he had handed me into the carriage. And just then, looking down at him, I had imagined that I might be able to go to her with an open mind, able to consider the possibility that she had somehow been made a victim.

But it was not easy to overcome the prejudice of years, and this morning I was full of all the old feelings of resentment. Yet I was prepared to make concessions. I would try to draw her out, try to discover what the truth behind the separation was.

The stone wall to our left finally terminated in a high iron gate which had been left open. There was a gatehouse, but its general state of disrepair seemed to indicate that it had been a long time since it had been lived in. For the first time it occurred to me to wonder just what financial provisions my father had made during the past sixteen years to keep Ludden Hall habitable. What a fool I had been not to insist that Mr. Harlow give me facts and figures concerning the upkeep of the estate before I had left London.

Certainly no money had been expended recently on the grounds, I thought as the coachman drove slowly up a gravel path which wound between thick rhododendron bushes which had obviously not been trimmed for many years. The park beyond seemed to be extensive although it was difficult to see for any distance due to the growth of saplings on either side of the path. If there had once been lawns and vistas, they were long since gone. Even the sun was shut out and there was a gloomy dankness about the approach which was unpleasant and did little to relieve my mood which now hovered on the brink of acute anxiety. Perhaps, I thought, I had been wrong not to let David come with me.

"Your father wouldn't know the place," Nelly said suddenly, sniffing. "It's a mercy he's gone to his grave."

I turned on her. "You've been here before?"

"Yes, and so have you," she replied with a bitterness I had never heard in her voice before. "Doubtless you were too young to remember, but we came here once when you were three. It was your mother who insisted on seeing the place. Lovely then, it was, all open spaces with the brushes pruned proper."

Perhaps there was no reason why she should have mentioned that she had come to Ludden Hall before, but I felt the same resentment I had felt the night before.

"Did we ever live here?" I asked with heavy irony. "Or would that be telling me more than it's good for me to know?"

Nelly ignored my tone. "We stayed the day and no longer," she replied tartly, "although there were servants and the place fit to be moved into. But it didn't suit your father to stay. He showed the house to your mother; just as she wanted, but that was as far as he would go, although she made a fuss about coming here for the summers. No doubt your father...."

"Had his reasons," I said in a low voice. "I wish he had been a bit freer with them."

"You're not to doubt him," Nelly said with sudden vehemence. "Now that he's not here to defend himself, I'll not let him be spoken ill of. Not by you, Miss, or by anyone. Although," she added ominously, "there'll be those willing enough to try."

"If you mean my mother," I began, "then I assume that...."

I broke off as the coach was reined to an abrupt halt. Shifting in my seat I leaned out the window, expecting to see the house. But we were still in the shadows of trees and bushes.

"What ho?" a thin voice cried, and an apparition appeared beside us in the form of a very old man seated in a Bath chair which was being rapidly propelled forward by a sullen-faced youth in shabby, grey livery.

"What ho?" the old man called again as the youth brought the chair to a stop beside the window from which I was leaning. Lord Ramsdale—for I was certain that it must be he—was wrapped in a plaid blanket, but an old-fashioned top hat was set jauntily on his head. Although his face was as emaciated as a skeleton's, his thin lips were twisted in a boyish grin and his pale blue eyes sparkled as he stared up at me.

"Pretty gel, ain't you?" he said without preamble. "Spitting image of your mother. See that you do better for yourself than she did, gel."

A muffled sound came from Nelly, but I had no time for her. Indeed the old man gave me no time to make any response. Drawing a withered hand from the blanket, he began to strike about himself with a gilt-headed cane.

"Come along, boy!" he exclaimed impatiently. "Open that carriage door and help me inside before I give you something to remember."

With surprising agility he hoisted himself from the Bath chair, blankets tumbling in every direction. But he was weak on his feet and would have fallen if the boy had not hurried to support him.

"Bloody servants!" he muttered between groans as he was hoisted onto the seat beside me. "Put me in the care of driveling idiots, will she?"

He flicked the cane at the boy who managed, just in time, to close the door between them. Keeping his head well below the open window, he handed in the blanket. Still speechless with amazement, I wrapped it about my grandfather's shoulders.

"Damned nuisance, age," the old man muttered, keeping a firm grip on the riding crop. "Now, let me look at you, gel. What's your name, eh? I forget names. Always have. Damned nuisance."

"I'm Ruth," I said.

"And I'm Lord Ramsdale," the old gentleman replied gleefully. "You can call me Bertie. All my friends call me Bertie."

I remembered what Professor Rankin had told me. This man had squandered away a fortune. He had always been an eccentric. And David had said that I would like him. I realized with relief that he delighted me. He was a true original, like no one I had ever met before.

His eyes flashed from me to Nelly who sat staring at him with ill concealed astonishment, her handkerchief to her lips.

"Who's this?" he demanded.

"This is Nelly. My nurse."

"Too old to have a nurse, gel," he muttered, inclining his head toward Nelly like a curious bird. "Nurse, is she? Then she can call me m'lord. Doesn't do to let menials get too far above themselves."

I shot Nelly a warning glance, but there was no need. She had withdrawn her handkerchief from her lips and her mouth appeared to have been sewn shut, although her eyes were dark with disapproval.

"What's the matter with the bloody horses?" my grandfather demanded. "Going to stand here all day, are they?" He leaned his head out the window. "Gee up!" he called in a voice like that of a feeble banshee.

The coach began to move and we passed the boy who was returning in the direction he had come, pushing the empty Bath chair. As we passed him, my grandfather waved his cane out the window and chuckled.

"She won't be pleased," he said in what I took to be a reference to my mother. "Wanted to pack me out of the way for the day, she did. But I fooled her. Thought she could keep me from seeing my own granddaughter, did she? Silly bitch!"

Nelly gasped, but I said nothing. For suddenly the carriage had swept around a curve in the drive and I saw Ludden Hall standing in the softly curved hollow below, a beautiful Tudor manor house with soft brick walls and twisted chimney pots.

"There it is, gel," the old man beside me said, gripping my arm with bony fingers. "Welcome home. You were a long time coming."

Chapter Three

OF ALL THE responses I had anticipated, delight had certainly not been one of them. But as the carriage rattled down the road which broadened to an avenue, I felt a rising sense of excitement. More than that. Happiness. The sun glinted on the mullioned panes of the old windows and the dew glistened on the ivy which clung to the time-mellowed walls. Incredibly I felt as though I were returning to a place I had long loved.

Beside me my grandfather kept silent, but I could feel his eyes on my face. It was impossible to disguise my delight. The house was a gem, as freshly minted as it had been when Elizabeth was queen. How could my father have kept it from me? His heritage. Mine.

Sheep grazed the grass before a low door set deep in the outer wall. The carriage came to a stop and the silence was broken only by the stamping of the horses' hooves and the low moaning call of doves nesting in the eaves.

"What price London, eh?" my grandfather said jauntily. "What price London?"

The words cut through my unexpected sense of happiness like a knife. My home was in London. The house in Sloan Square. My father's beautiful furniture. His books. How could I have forgotten, even for a moment? This was no homecoming. My father had rejected Ludden Hall. For reasons I knew nothing of. But for good reasons. Surely he would never have sent me here if he had thought....

Or had he known that I would love it? As once he must have done before his parents died. Even when he was a boy, such beauty could not have been lost on him. He had spent his life relishing relics of the past. And yet this manor house which should have been his greatest treasure....

"She won't be coming out to make you welcome," the old man said. "Not her."

I shook my head, reluctant to let my train of thought be broken. My father had trained me to value the beauty of the past above everything. He must have known that once I had seen Ludden Hall, I would never want to leave it.

It was a mad thought. I could see Nelly watching me curiously. But I could not pretend that nothing was wrong. What if my father *had* guessed my reaction? If he had not charged me with the delivery of the box and the letter, I might not have come here for years. In an attempt to avoid meeting my mother, I could have arranged for Mr. Harlow to see to the managing of the estate. But my father had made certain that I would come here. Why? Because he hoped that I might want

Ludden Hall so desperately that I would turn away my mother?

I shook my head to clear my mind. For some reason I remembered what Nelly had said when I had first told her we were coming here. "Evil," she had cried. But the woman I had still not seen was not responsible for the thoughts that forced themselves on me now. I was responsible for my own disloyalty.

"She may pretend differently, but she's afraid of you, gel," my grandfather declared. "Don't you be taken in. Bullies are bloody cowards. Ought to know. Never was a greater bully than I was as a lad. Who's this?"

The coachman, having clambered down from his perch, was holding open the carriage door. His face impassive, he ignored my grandfather's mutterings and helped him to the ground. Nelly and I followed.

"See that you call me m'lord," my grandfather warned the coachman as he leaned against him for support. His blanket had been left behind him in the carriage, and I saw that he was wearing a morning coat which might have fitted him in years past, but now hung vacantly about his shoulders. His trousers were green with age and of an unfashionable cut. Still, the top hat was set at a rakish angle on his white hair and somehow there was nothing absurd about him.

"Pull the rope there," he was telling the coachman, flicking his cane impatiently. "Pull it, man! I want my dram of whiskey. It's past time. Past time."

The man pulled the rope hanging at the side of the iron-bolted coach door and a great clamor of bells shattered the silence. Almost at once the door was pulled open, creaking on its hinges.

"This is Mallick," my grandfather declared. "At least that's what he chooses to call himself."

The man servant who stood before us was wearing the uniform of a butler. He was a thickset man with a hairline so low as to make his face apelike. As he stood aside to let us pass, I was aware of a sense of hostility.

My grandfather flicked his cane at him.

"My lord," Mallick muttered.

"Louder, you bloody idiot," the old man said conversationally.

"M'LORD."

"That's better. Go tell your mistress that her guests have arrived. And fetch me my whiskey to the drawing room. She won't fuss about my tipple today. Too much else on her mind."

Mallick led the way up a path which bisected a small courtyard warm with sunlight where roses had been allowed to run wild. The house embraced the courtyard, two stories high on three sides. The very air seemed fragrant with age. I knew I should be thinking of the meeting which lay ahead, but I could think of nothing except that all of this was mine.

Another low door and we were inside the house itself. To the right stretched a wide room which once must have been the great hall, the walls dark with oak paneling and a great, gaping fireplace, empty and cold. What furniture there was—a long refectory table and several chairs—were of the same vintage as the house. Some ragged banners were suspended from the wall beneath the minstrel's gallery. A dim painting hung above the mantel. Everything was thick with dust.

My grandfather's strength was clearly waning, although he continued to urge the coachman on with a variety of insults. Crossing the hall, we found ourselves in a sunlit chamber which had doubtlessly once been the retiring room for the ladies of my Elizabethan ancestors. The thought gave me pleasure, but the room itself did not. Just as the jewels were vulgar, so were the furnishings here. Ugly horsehair couches were crowded in corners and tables covered with fringed cloth and various ornaments cluttered the room. Every piece seemed to have been chosen as a deliberate exercise in bad taste except for a single linen-covered easy chair into which my grandfather was lowering himself.

"You may wait outside," I told the coachman as Mallick reappeared with a glass and a bottle set on a silver tray. With a sigh of contentment my grandfather watched him pour the drink, and then accepted the glass with a steady hand.

"Quite right," he said, leering his approval at the butler. "First things first. Now tell your mistress she is keeping her guests waiting."

He peered inquiringly at Nelly over the brim of his glass, and she stared back at him from the shelter of her bonnet.

"Perhaps," my grandfather said to me, "this one would like to go to the kitchen. Have Cook give her a cup of tea. That sort of thing. Or perhaps I'm being old fashioned. My daughter often says that I'm old fashioned."

"I'd rather have Nelly stay," I said. The vulgarity of the room had brought me back to reality and I remembered the jewel box. I had the letter in my beaded purse, but I had forgotten to bring the box from the carriage.

And then I saw that Nelly was carrying it and I smiled my thanks. A scowl was my reply.

"Unpleasant creature, ain't she?" my grandfather demanded conventionally. "Sit down, gel. Sit down. Liberty hall, that's what this is. How do you fancy this room? Outfitted it herself, your mother did. Do the whole place over the same way if she had the funds. No more taste than the bloody queen. Makes me glad I squandered my own money instead of leaving her to do it for me. Your father was wise to provide for her modestly. Between the two of us...." He broke off laughing like a rusty hinge.

I took a chair close beside him and smiled, wondering if he ever restrained himself from saying precisely what he thought.

"Guts," he continued, waving his now empty glass around aimlessly. "You'll need em, gel. You'll need em."

I took the glass from him and set it on one of the numerous round tables which seemed to surround me.

"I met David last night, grandfather," I said. "He told me that I would like you and I do."

The old man preened himself.

"Call me Bertie," he said for the second time. "Pretty gels always take a fancy to me. I remember when I was twenty. . . ."

He broke off, staring past me. Suddenly his eyes seemed hooded.

"What on earth are you doing here, Father?"

It was a low, firm, commanding voice. Turning in my chair, I saw the woman standing in the doorway.

Although I had been forewarned, the sight of her shook me. It was like looking into the future, for there was my thick, auburn hair faded by time. There was my face with the cheekbones starkly prominent. And there were my eyes, less thickly fringed, perhaps. More deeply set. But surely I had never looked at anyone in such an extraordinary way, with such a dull impassive expression behind which distaste seemed to lurk.

Out of the corner of my eye I saw Nelly back toward the door, clutching the red plush box to her bosom as though someone were about to snatch it away from her. Even my grandfather's pertness disappeared and he seemed to shrink in his chair.

"So," my mother said in a heavy voice, slowly coming toward me. "You are Ruth."

She moved gracefully enough, but somehow I was reminded of a sleepwalker as she swayed toward me. Rich lace encircled her long neck and slender wrists. She might have been receiving a slight acquaintance to her home as she came to stand beside my chair. Her smile—for she *did* smile—was gracious. But her eyes... I could not meet them. They promised to tell me that it was true that she hated me.

I tried to brace myself with the memory of what David had told me. It was possible that she could have been a victim sixteen years ago. I remembered, too, what the old man had told me only minutes before. Perhaps she was afraid, despite her relaxed appearance. I was a stranger to her and perhaps it was not her fault that it was so. I came here as owner of Ludden Hall, and she had every reason to be afraid. Still, I could not be soft with her—let her hurt me. I had promised myself that I would come to her as a woman and not a child.

"Yes," I said. "I am Ruth."

For a moment those strange eyes seemed intent on tracing every line of my face. And then she turned and pulled a bell rope by the fireplace. Mallick reappeared so quickly that I knew he must have been waiting just outside the door.

"Take Lord Ramsdale to his room," my mother said. "And later I will want to speak to the boy. He had orders from me which, apparently, he disobeyed."

"The lad did as I told him," my grandfather muttered, and I realized they were speaking of the sullen youth who had pushed my Bath chair. "Needed my constitutional," my grandfather added.

My mother picked up the empty glass from the chair where I had set it and sniffed.

"Is this your doing, Mallick?" she asked.

There was no expression in her voice, and Mallick

replied in kind.

"His lordship ordered me to serve him, Madam," he said.

"I am the only person who gives orders, Mallick. I...."

Her voice faltered, and I wondered if she was recalling the fact that what she had said was not technically true.

"We'll see, lass," my grandfather grumbled, apparently following the same line of thought. "We'll see."

Still, he allowed Mallick to assist him from the chair.

"Remember what I told you, gel," he said to me with some of his former jauntiness as he was helped from the room.

"You must pay no attention to my father," my mother said in that slow, deliberate voice when he was gone. "As you must have realized, he is in his dotage."

Since the old man had struck me as being anything but senile, I did not respond. My mother was no longer smiling.

"I see you have brought Nelly," she said in that slow, dreamlike voice.

She moved to the fireplace and assumed what seemed to me to be quite a deliberate pose with one arm resting on the mantel.

"Yes," I said, finding that my mouth was dry. "She has something for you."

My mother arched her eyebrows.

"Indeed."

I nodded to Nelly as she advanced hesitantly, her eyes lowered, and presented the red plush box.

If the sight of it startled my mother, she gave no sign.

"Ah yes," she said. "My jewels. Put them on the table, Nelly."

I rose and took the extended box. "There is an

inventory inside," I said, "signed by Mr. Harlow and my father sixteen years ago. Perhaps you would like to check the contents against it."

"There is no need," my mother assured me in a disinterested voice. "Whatever interest I once had in the 'contents,' as you refer to them, has long since passed."

Somehow she managed to infer that she had as little interest in me as she had in the jewels.

"There is a letter, as well," I said, taking the envelope from my beaded purse. "I was commissioned by the terms of my father's will to deliver it to you personally."

She took the letter from me. Our fingers did not touch.

"Have you any other 'commissions'?" she asked.

It was a clear dismissal. In my daydreams this was the moment when I should leave, head held high. Not, perhaps, without asking to see the estate agent. And yet . . .

I could not—would not—leave this house without a discussion of the future. Now that I had seen Ludden Hall I knew that I could not stay away from it indefinitely. It would be a coward's work to return to London and direct Mr. Harlow to send a letter stating that she must make her home elsewhere, since I had decided to make Ludden Hall my home.

And yet that was what I had determined. I realized that now.

Cowards were bullies. That was what my grandfather had said.

"I think," I murmured, "that we must discuss the future."

Her face grew pale.

"Very well."

Some sort of preliminary skirmish had been fought and won. And I was victor.

"Sit down, Nelly," I said, assuming the role of hostess. "Perhaps we could have tea."

When my mother made no move, I walked across the room and pulled the bell rope. We waited in silence until a young maid appeared, scurrying in the door like a frightened rabbit.

I waited for my mother to give the order and when she did not, I said, "We will have tea."

The girl gave one frightened look at the figure by the fireplace, but my mother's face might have been carved of ivory.

"At once, if you please," I added.

"And show this woman to the kitchen," my mother said suddenly in a harsh voice. "She will take tea there."

"No," I said firmly as Nelly began to move toward the door. "This lady will take her tea with us."

"As you will." My mother shrugged her slim shoulders.

"Yes," I said as the maid scurried from the room. "As I will."

My mother smiled, but this time she seemed genuinely amused, although the strange, dull expression in her eyes did not change.

"You are very like your father, I see."

"I am like myself," I told her, "and there are questions to be asked and answered."

"How astute of you," she mocked me.

"I met my stepbrother last night. At least I assume that is our relationship."

"Did you, indeed."

She pretended to be unsurprised, but I found that I could sense her change of mood as though it were not only a face we shared. She was wary now.

"He told me certain things which came as a surprise to me," I told her.

Again she shrugged. "I expect there are many things

which would surprise you."

I was aware of a growing irritation. I did not intend to thrust and parry with her indefinitely.

"Perhaps," I said, "you would do me the kindness of reading the letter before we proceed."

For a moment I thought she meant to refuse, and then her shoulders slumped.

"As you will," she said again.

Slitting open the envelope with her fingernail, she unfolded the letter inside. I looked at Nelly. There was an expression of warning in her eyes, and I guessed that she thought it would be better had we left.

And then my mother gave a low cry. The letter fell to the floor. There were two sheets of paper and I could see, even from a distance, that each was written in a different hand. One was my father's spidery scrawl. And the other. . . .

My mother bent to pick the pages up and then sank into a chair.

"Very well," she said in a voice grown thin and shrill. "What do you want of me?"

"The truth," I said.

It was then that she began to laugh. Leaning back against the chair and arching her graceful neck, she laughed until tears came to her eyes.

The laughter stopped as abruptly as it had begun when the little maid hurried back into the room carrying a tray laden with Royal Worcester china of a particularly garish red and green design. For a moment the girl seemed confused as to where to set the tray and I gestured toward the low table before my mother's chair.

Apparently in firm control of herself, she poured. Cups in hand, we sat in silence for a moment, looking at one another thoughtfully. Nelly permitted herself a sip of tea and then sat staring at the floor.

"Where do you wish to begin?" my mother said finally in a wintery voice. "Assuming that you know the contents of these two letters. . . ."

"I know nothing of the contents," I told her. "Mr. Harlow delivered the envelope to me sealed, and even if it had not been, I would never have opened it."

Her lips curled in bitter amusement. "I see that your father imparted all his virtues to you," she said. "A pity, that. Explanations would have been easier if you had read them. Perhaps you would like to do so now."

"I think not," I murmured.

A strange sense of unreality had overtaken me. The events of the morning had been so unlike what I had expected. The meeting with my grandfather and the affinity which had somehow been established between us. The strength of my response to the house itself. My own unexpected decision to learn something more of the past. Only my mother's hostility had not taken me by surprise. And now, through my own doing, I had put myself in the position of questioner. And I was not certain what questions to ask.

"What is it, precisely, that you want to know?" my mother said, and now her voice was somehow heavier than ever before.

I looked at Nelly and saw her shake her head. She thought I was making a mistake, obviously. Probably she was eager for us to leave. There was no reason why she should understand the way I felt. But if she thought that I was yielding to some sentimental desire to establish intimacy with the marble-faced woman sitting opposite me, she was mistaken.

"Last night," I said slowly, "David implied that you did not—abandon me voluntarily."

"Abandon," she said slowly. "Is that how your father described it?"

"On the contrary," I told her, eager to make myself

clear. "He never spoke of the circumstances of your leaving the house at Sloan Square."

"And you never asked."

It was a condemnation.

"I must have when you first left. But I have no memory now of what explanation my father gave me. However, I am certain that he never used the word 'abandon.'"

"I find it difficult to believe that you never pressed the matter when you were older."

Her eyes were like blue steel veiled with fog.

"I think I must have sensed that he did not want to talk about it."

"You must have believed that I did not want to see you again."

"Yes," I admitted. "What other assumption could I make given the fact that you never made any attempt to contact me in any way."

"Those were the terms," my mother said in a low voice. "I had no choice."

I took a deep breath. "Are you accusing my father of deliberately keeping you from me?"

"Of course." She spoke as though it were a simple and obvious fact.

"He would never have been that cruel," I protested, rising. "I refuse to believe that of him. I want to know the truth, not...."

"Lies? I assure you that I am misrepresenting nothing. I may not be as honorable as you and your father, but I have nothing to gain by lying about this. Nelly can verify that when I left London I was in no position to protest any terms your father wished to make."

"Is it true, Nelly?" I demanded.

"It was no concern of mine, Miss Ruth." Nelly's eyes pleaded with me.

"You can't deny that you were in the next room the

night he found out," my mother said with sudden vehemence, quite unlike her former laconic pronouncements. "You must have heard something of · what was said. On that and other occasions. They were the few times he raised his voice."

I remembered my earlier suspicions.

"Did it have anything to do with those bits of jewelry?" I said, indicating the red plush box.

"You're very shrewd, aren't you?" my mother replied slowly. "Yes. To be exact it had to do with the gentleman who gave them to me. Since you want the truth, you shall have it. He was my lover."

To suspect was one thing. To know, another. Suddenly I felt chilled. And tired. Incredibly tired.

"His name is beside the point," my mother said, aiming each word at me like a dart. "He was a friend of my father. Much younger, but a friend. Very like my first husband. I told your father that. I tried to warn him."

"Warn him?"

"Oh, he was so naive. Intelligent but naive. He didn't care for the things I liked. Plays. Going about in society. I can't imagine why he married me. Probably I was the only mistake he ever made. He gave in to me about leaving Oxford. But even in London I was suffocating. Not that that really mattered to your father. He only wanted not to be bothered. And so—I never bothered him. The gentleman I spoke of was glad enough to act as my escort. Any other man except your father would have seen where it was leading."

There was a hint of weary triumph in her smile. No doubt she hoped to shock me, and perhaps she had. But I had long since guessed that something very serious must have gone wrong between her and my father. No, on the whole I was far from shocked. In fact I felt relieved. Because what she had told me absolved my father. There was no need for me to doubt him. As

Professor Rankin had suggested, he had acted reasonably. And more than fairly for, although adultery was not sufficient grounds for a woman to divorce a man, it was quite enough when brought as evidence against a wife to allow the marriage ties to be expeditiously unknotted.

My mother was waiting. Expectant. I sensed that. And I determined not to give her the satisfaction of an immediate response. Certainly I was not about to offer her sympathy. Perhaps she had been left lonely. But she must have known when she married my father that he was not the sort of person who enjoyed idle entertainment and wasted hours over tea cups.

What on earth, I wondered, had brought them together? It would be easier to believe that this woman wanted security at any cost. Apparently her first husband's death had left her with little income. And, as Professor Rankin had said, her father had by that time lost his own fortune and was living in rented houses, entertaining a motley group of friends. Many of them, no doubt, with futures no more promising than his. My father must have stood out in a group like that, he and the other dons from Oxford who came out of curiosity and because Lord Ramsdale set a good table.

Yes, that was likely to be the answer. As long as I had known him, my father had shied from women. Perhaps when he met my mother he had become the victim of his own inexperience, in spite of the fact that he had been over forty at the time. If that were the case, then it followed that she might have lured him into marriage with the usual inducements. She did not strike me as the scrupulous sort. In fact her story of why she and my father had separated had made that clear. But in the beginning she must have managed to convince him that they would be happy in spite of the lack of any intellectual intercourse. It must have troubled him to see that even though he had given up his life as a scholar and come to London that was not enough for her. Doubtlessly when she had presented him with her father's young friend as someone quite willing to escort her here and there, my father had been relieved. He must have trusted her or he would never have permitted the relationship to develop. And she had betrayed his trust. It was as simple as that. A sordid story, but not an uncommon one.

"Perhaps," my mother said heavily, "I have been too frank. After all, you are only a girl and I expect you have led a very sheltered life. I can see that Nelly is shocked that I should speak so openly to you, but you wanted the truth and you have had it."

I resisted the temptation to take issue with her on the matter of my having been sheltered since I doubted whether she would understand that there was as much to be learned between the covers of a book as in the press and flurry of the ballroom. History was full of stories such as the one she had just told me, and my father, whatever she might think, had never kept me from reading anything I cared to read. But she was right about Nelly's reaction. I saw outrage written clearly on the face of the older woman, and, for a moment, I was afraid that she might blurt out her opinion. She had called my mother evil once. This might be the moment for her to utter the word again.

"I'm glad you have been so honest with me," I said quickly to ward off any such interruption. "Can I assume that once the—discovery was made my father suggested that you leave the house at Sloan Square?"

"He demanded, he did not suggest," my mother said with slow bitterness. "Or, to put it more plainly, he threatened. Unless I retired to the country, he told me that he would obtain a divorce. I was not to see you again as long as you were a child, and, whatever you may care to believe, that was unutterably painful to me. But then, of course, I have had sixteen years to recover."

I realized that she was making it quite clear that whatever she had once felt for me was gone. She wanted no display of emotion. David had told me that she had changed. Was this what he meant? Was it possible that what had happened to her meant that she was no longer capable of feeling? If so, she was greatly to be pitied. But how could I pity her? How could I feel any sympathy for someone who had betrayed the one person I had ever loved?

"What about the gentleman?" I said coldly. "Your friend. You risked a good deal for him. I would have thought. . . ."

"That we should have gone away together?" My mother smiled dreamily. "What an innocent you are. His career would have been ruined by the scandal. Unlike your father he had no private fortune. I had no choice but to come here. No choice but to take my own father in when he reached the end of his resources."

"You had David."

"I'll thank you not to list my consolations for me," my mother murmured. "This place has been a prison and your father kept the keys in the form of this case of jewelry and this letter. Both were proof of my infidelity. As long as they were in his keeping, there was no chance for me to take my revenge."

Something in her voice chilled me.

"What sort of revenge?" I demanded.

Again that twisted smile.

"You will know soon enough," she told me. "All of England will know soon enough. Perhaps it never occurred to you to wonder why your father was willing enough to let me make this place my home, why he never set foot on the grounds unless it was absolutely necessary, even before we married."

There was an answer to another question here. I *had* wondered. But now I did not want to know. I put my hand on Nelly's shoulder and she rose.

"Perhaps I should give you a hint of my intentions," my mother said in a low voice. She was staring past me and her mouth was twisted in what might have been a ghastly smile or an expression of pain.

"You have no power to do anything which should concern me," I told her. "And my father is dead. There is nothing you can do to hurt him now."

"I can destroy his reputation," my mother murmured. "I can expose him for the murderer that he was. More than that. I can provide an heir to his entire estate. This house. His fortune. Everything. And now, leave. I have nothing more to say to you. But when you return to London, I suggest you see your solicitor. You will need to think of ways to protect yourself."

Chapter Four

"YOU SHOULDN'T HAVE GONE, Miss Ruth. I knew no good would come of it."

I shook my head wearily. If Nelly had said that once since we had left Ludden Hall, she had said it a hundred times. I had scarcely heard her at first, so intent was I in peering out the carriage window to engrave the memory of the house on my mind as the horses paced their way up the winding drive. But now I was tired and impatient. The return trip to London had been exhausting. The threats which my mother had made had frightened me. It was all very well for Nelly to tell me that it was obvious the woman was deranged. For myself I was not so certain. For sixteen years her hatred had festered. There was no doubt in my mind that she would go to any length to ruin my father's name, to strip me of his inheritance.

In vain I tried to recall anything that might cast some light on the matter. Once my father had mentioned an elder brother, but I only knew that he had died long before I was born. Professor Rankin had mentioned a tragedy. But my mother had spoken of murder.

It made no sense. Whatever the circumstances of my uncle's death, there was no heir. I would have known if that were so. Ludden Hall and the fortune would never have passed to my father. But it had. And now, legally, everything belonged to me. Mr. Harlow had told me so. I had seen the documents.

And yet....

There had been a message waiting for me when I reached the house at Sloan Square at midnight, an urgent message from Mr. Harlow himself asking me to come to his office the following day.

Had it not been for sheer emotional exhaustion, I would never have slept. The next morning, gloved and bonneted, I left the house by cab. I could not think logically, although I tried as we proceeded down streets crowded with carriages and carts of every variety on our way to the Strand where Mr. Harlow had offices at the Inns of Court.

His clerk, a sallow faced young man who made little attempt to conceal his curiosity, ushered me at once into the inner office. It was only necessary for me to take one look at Mr. Harlow's face to know that something was very wrong indeed.

"My dear Miss Bramwell," he said, rising. "How pale you look. Sit down. Sit down. I am afraid that you have heard the news already. Believe me, if I had known—if I had even guessed—I would have kept you from making the journey to Ludden Hall. You must believe that this has come as great a shock to me as it has to you."

"I know nothing," I told him stiffly, displeased by his flood of words which served only to heighten my fears. "My mother made certain threats. . . . But I cannot believe that there was any truth in them."

The desk between the solicitor and me seemed a great distance for, despite the look of concern on his plump face, he seemed, somehow, to have retreated from me. There was a certain wariness in his eyes, an air of caution which I had never noticed before. Perhaps this disturbed me more than anything else.

"Will you be so kind as to tell me precisely what your mother told you?" he said.

"What does it matter?" I replied. "The only thing that is clear is that I know very little of my father's past. You could have told me, at least, that my mother was married before she married my father. And that she has a stepson. *And* a father. My grandfather. How could you have let me go to Ludden Hall so—so unprepared?"

Leaning back in his chair, Mr. Harlow folded his hands on his waistcoat and assumed an air of outraged dignity.

"I assure you, Miss Bramwell," he said, "that I had no idea that you had not been told the details of intimate family relationships. The thought never entered my mind!"

I gripped my gloved hands tight together. It was clearly no time to level accusations. If anyone was to be blamed for my ignorance, it was my father. The time had come when I had to accept that.

"Very well," I said. "But from this moment on, you will do me the favor of assuming that I know nothing. Whatever you have to tell me, keep that in mind. For some reason I have been kept in complete ignorance of my own family's affairs. It is, I assure you, an intolerable situation. If I have offended you because of the—the pressure I feel I am under, my apologies."

"Yes, yes, of course," Mr. Harlow replied, something of his old manner returning. "The fact is, my dear, we find ourselves in a difficult situation."

I waited with ill-disguised impatience, moving restlessly in my chair.

A gentleman called on me yesterday," Mr. Harlow continued. "But perhaps it would be better for me to begin with certain events which happened more than twenty years before you were born."

He cleared his throat.

"My father represented the Bramwell estate then, but when I succeeded him, he told me what he knew of the family—your family, my dear. Not for the purpose of gossip, of course, but simply because a solicitor should know...."

I nodded impatiently.

"Your paternal grandfather was a country gentleman of the old school," Mr. Harlow went on, fingering his gold watch chain nervously. "He and his wife had two sons. Your father was the youngest. His brother, Harry, was ten years his senior. But, of course, you know...."

"I know there was a brother and that he died," I said. "Nothing more."

"It was a great tragedy," the solicitor went on rapidly. "Your father was seventeen at the time and in his last year at Eton. He had, I believe, already shown a certain scholarly inclination and was being prepared to go up to Oxford. His elder brother shared the country interests of his father and lived at Ludden Hall. It was assumed that he would take your grandfather's place in running the estate. And then the accident occurred."

My mother had spoken of murder. But I would not repeat the word, not even to this man whom I trusted.

"The brother, Harry, drowned while fishing in the

river which runs through the grounds of the estate,"
Mr. Harlow said.

I took a deep breath. It was a tragedy, of course, but
one which happened every day. If it had been a matter
of a gun shot...

"Was my father with him?" I asked.

Mr. Harlow glanced at me curiously.

"Yes. I remember clearly my father telling me of the
desperate attempts made to save Harry. But it was
useless. Your father dragged his brother from the river,
but there was nothing to be done. They were very close,
and I believe that your father nearly suffered a
complete breakdown afterward. As for the parents,
they never recovered from their loss. Your grandfather
fell into a decline and died of a heart seizure shortly
afterward. His wife, I believe, had always been delicate
and it surprised no one when her death followed later
the same year."

I shuddered. No wonder my father had never
spoken of this. No wonder he had returned to Ludden
Hall as rarely as possible, even while he was still at
Oxford. And yet my mother had dared to speak of
murder. It was clear to me now that, in her bitterness,
she had taken the past and woven another pattern to it.
Her own son had told me that she had changed. And
Nelly had told me that she was deranged. I was willing
to believe it now.

And then I remembered how Mr. Harlow had
begun this interview.

"The gentleman who came to see you," I said
quickly. "I suppose he is some unscrupulous lawyer
hired by my mother."

Again that curious expression came into the
solicitor's eyes.

"What did she say that would lead you to believe
that she would hire anyone?" he began.

"It doesn't matter what she said to me," I told him.

"What—what accusations did this man make?"

"I'm afraid he made no accusation, although from what you have said, I fear that this will be a more serious matter than I had guessed. You see, my dear, he made a claim."

"A claim?"

There was a fire burning in the grate, but I was chilled to the bone. I pulled my cape more closely about me.

"He claims to be your uncle's son," Mr. Harlow said slowly. "A—er, legitimate son. If that were not the case there would be no problem from our point of view. But he brought certain papers with him—papers of which he had only lately learned the importance."

"What sort of papers?"

"A copy of a marriage certificate," the solicitor said heavily. "A record of Harry Bramwell's marriage to a certain Grace Evans. And another document which he claims to be a record of his birth, three months after your uncle drowned. The fact of the matter is, my dear, that if his claims can be supported, he and not you is the heir to Ludden Hall and everything else besides."

I took a hansom cab as far as Kensington Gardens. It was a brisk October day, full of sun and wind. The water of the Serpentine was a mirror for the cloudless sky and late roses bloomed along the winding walks. I scarcely noticed. Not until I reached the new memorial which the queen had ordered erected to Prince Albert did I pause. It was a magnificent structure rising nearly two hundred feet into the air, and I stood looking up at the statue of the prince seated under an elaborately decorated stone canopy, remembering other days when I had passed by this place with my father.

"Something in the Greek tradition would have been more appropriate," he had always said, scowling at the elaborately sculptured base where the four quarters of the globe were represented by masses of bas relief. "Still, I suppose the lady has the right to set the style for tastelessness. Other monarchs have done worse violence to the country."

For a moment it was as though I could hear his voice, and it was with an effort that I reminded myself that I would never again hear him state his opinion on anything. What judgement I had inherited from him I would keep. Beyond that . . .

Feeling lost I sank down on a bench and tried to concentrate on the passing parade of men in morning coats and ladies with their trailing skirts and feathered bonnets. But it was a vain attempt to cling to reality. My inner focus had shifted. Try as I might, I knew that from now on I could only concern myself with the past.

I began with the last hour. Had I allowed it, Mr. Harlow would have told me as little as possible about Jason Bramwell, the man who had claimed to be my cousin and heir to the fortune I had thought was mine. But I had insisted on being told everything, and the story which had followed had disconcerted me.

According to the claimant—for so I had determined to call him in my mind—my father's elder brother, Harry, had fallen in love with the daughter of the estate agent at Ludden Hall, a girl named Grace Evans, and had gotten her with child. A secret marriage had taken place and Harry had promised to make the union public. But he delayed too long, and before her lying-in, his young wife had found herself a widow.

"Mr.—er, Bramwell was not too clear concerning what followed," Mr. Harlow had told me, "since it seems that even when he came of age his mother insisted on remaining vague on the subject. But apparently her father went to your grandfather soon after Harry's funeral and demanded a settlement. That was provided only when Evans promised to take his daughter and the child to Canada."

And that was where they had gone, settling in Nova Scotia. According to the claimant he had been educated there and become an architect.

"His mother died ten years ago when he was thirty," Mr. Harlow had told me. "Old Evans was long since dead. Mr. Bramwell claims to have known nothing of his heritage, except that his father was dead. It came as a complete surprise to him when, two months ago, he received a letter from your mother."

So she was behind it all. I suppose it should not have shocked me, knowing, as I did, the depth of her bitterness. But the thought that she had gone to the trouble of digging up an old scandal had horrified me. But even as I had tried to express myself, Mr. Harlow reminded me that all might not be as it seemed.

"If such a substantial financial settlement had been made," he had told me, "my father would have been aware of it. I must have time to go through old records. Remember this, my dear Ruth. This Jason Bramwell has a good deal to gain. Fortunes such as yours attract certain types of men. It may be that he and your mother are in some sort of criminal collusion. He insisted on leaving his papers with me, and at some time or other they must be authenticated. We may well find that this is much ado about nothing."

I had found myself grasping at straws. Did the claimant bear a family resemblance? And once I had asked the question I had realized the irony of it, for there was nothing of my father about my face. My mother had left too clear a mark upon it. Why should not Grace Evans have done the same?

"Since I never knew your uncle," Mr. Harlow had replied, "that is difficult to tell. I have been able to establish this, however. There was a man named George Evans employed at Ludden Hall as estate agent when your father and his brother were young men.

And Evans did leave your grandfather's employ and emigrate to Canada."

It was damning evidence. Hand in hand with a legal marriage and birth certificate, it meant the end of everything I had thought life held for me. Perhaps if I had never seen Ludden Hall I would not have responded so passionately. The luxury of my life at the house in Sloan Square meant little to me. Under other circumstances I would have been content to earn my living as an antiquarian. Taken pride in it, in fact. But to lose that house . . .

No, there was more to it than that, I reminded myself, staring at a nodding bed of asters. My mother had talked of murder. She had brought this man back to England not simply for the purpose of taking an estate from me. She meant to prove, somehow, that my father had killed his own brother in order to become heir.

The carriages rattled past Queen's Gate, opposite, but the traffic blurred before my eyes. I had asked Mr. Harlow if there had been any other claim made by this man who called himself Jason Bramwell, and he had told me no.

"But if you suspect something. . . ." he had said.

I could not tell him. There was one hope in my mind and that was that my mother had fabricated this claim and that, despite her threat to me, it would go no further. I was willing to accept the possibility that my father's brother had gotten Grace Evans with child. But he need not have married her. The papers the claimant had brought with him to England might well be forgeries. Perhaps he had acted in good faith. Or perhaps he had connived with my mother to deprive me of my heritage. But he might not know that there was more to follow. That a charge of murder might be made.

I felt driven as the leaves overhead. How could I

return to Sloan Square and wait for Mr. Harlow to follow legal channels? With Ludden Hall at stake? My father's reputation?

Rising from the bench, I descended the stone steps to the street and hailed a passing cab. My father had followed the path of reason. But I was dealing with an irrational woman. A woman who would stop at nothing. Mr. Harlow had told me that the man who called himself Jason Bramwell was staying at Brown's Hotel. It was only a short distance. But even if it had been a hundred miles, I would have gone there. I was through with innuendo. I would talk to the man himself. And only then would I decide what course I would take.

We met in one of the waiting rooms of the hotel in an atmosphere of draped windows and tables which would have well suited my mother's taste. Jason Bramwell was a handsome man of over forty, well tailored and broad of shoulder. There was nothing of my father in the tanned face and for that I was relieved. But it meant nothing. This man claimed to be my uncle's child, and for that I had no point of reference. For the first time I realized how strange it was that I had never seen a portrait of any member of my father's family. For all I knew this man might be the image of my uncle. Not for the first time in the past few days I cursed my ignorance.

He showed no surprise at seeing me. Indeed, he behaved as though we had long been friends.

"Will you call me Jason?" he said easily. "And may I call you Ruth? I was just going in to luncheon. Perhaps you will join me."

I do not know what I had expected. A sinister personality, perhaps. A declared enemy. Certainly not this undeniable gentleman, with only a hint of accent to give evidence of the country of his birth.

It was an absurd situation, I told myself, and one of which Nelly would have strongly disapproved. But I had determined to follow instinct and so it was that the man who claimed to be my cousin and I found ourselves settled opposite one another at a small table in the embrasure of a bay window.

"Since I had no knowledge that I had a relative in this country until a short time ago," he said once the waiter had disappeared, "you must pardon me if I say that you are a delightful surprise."

I armed myself against his compliments. It would only make matters more difficult if I acknowledged that he was not only handsome but charming. Still it would have been ungracious of me not to incline my head. To smile.

"You must be surprised to see me here," I said. "Let me tell you at once that I came on impulse and that I am not at all certain that I followed the right course."

"I understand," he said.

Never had I met with such apparent sympathy. My father had always demanded reasons for my actions. But I had presented myself unexpectedly and with no better explanation than that I had come on impulse and yet he claimed to understand.

"I met with Mr. Harlow this morning," I said with what I hoped was a certain crispness. "He told me what he knew, but...."

"That was not enough for you." His eyes traced the lines of my face. "I realize that this has come as a great surprise to you. And I hope that you will believe that I would never have come to England if it had not been for a letter."

"From my mother?"

"I do not perfectly understand the situation yet," he said, sipping the wine the waiter poured and nodding his approval. "I received a letter from a place called

Ludden Hall in August. The woman who wrote to me claimed herself to be an aunt. She informed me that my father, of whom my mother had told me little, had been heir to an estate which his brother had been administering for nearly forty years. She added that my uncle, your father, was ill and not expected to recover. She did not mention your existence, but even if she had, I admit that my curiosity was aroused. She gave me Mr. Harlow's address and urged me to come to England to claim—and I think I quote her exactly— 'what was mine.'"

"Nothing more?" I murmured, wondering if it was possible that she had not written on murder as well. But perhaps she had been afraid that he would think her mad and not come if that word had been mentioned. The thought had no sooner crossed my mind than I realized that I was accepting his word that he *was* my cousin. I could not believe that until it was proved. For all I knew, despite his apparent sincerity, he could be an agent hired for the purpose of defrauding me. Or, at the least, an illegitimate son who had provided himself with false papers.

"Nothing more," he said earnestly. "I put it to you. Under like circumstances, would you have responded as I have? Come to England?"

"Perhaps," I said.

"But of course you must consider me suspect," he went on. "I quite understand that. As Mr. Harlow must have warned you, until the documents I brought with me are authenticated, you have every right to suspect me."

I found myself wishing that he did not have so direct a gaze.

"I did not understand the true state of affairs until I talked to your solicitor," he went on. "And when I did, I realized that I had entered a hornet's nest."

He was too direct. I had not expected this sort of

confrontation. It was impossible to ask him if his credentials were real or forged—impossible to form a conclusion.

"Have you—have you talked with my mother?" I said as the waiter set bowls of soup before us.

"No," he replied. "I only arrived here on Tuesday. I went directly to Harlow. It was obvious that I took him by surprise. He tried to make the situation clear to me, but I confess to still being confused. It appears that after my father's death and the subsequent death of my—our—grandfather, your father became heir."

"There was no reason for him to be otherwise," I said stiffly.

"No, I'm sure not, since apparently no one on this side of the Atlantic was aware of my existence."

Our eyes met.

"Your existence is still in question," I said in a low voice.

He inclined his head. "It is quite natural that you should feel as you do," he said. "I gather that this has been a particularly difficult time for you."

"My father died," I said, "leaving all sorts of questions unanswered."

"You must understand this," Jason said slowly. "I did not come to England with the intention of robbing you of what you quite naturally believe to be your inheritance. As I said, until I met with Mr. Harlow yesterday, I was not aware of you either."

"My mother's letter...."

"She did not mention you. I take it from what Mr. Harlow said that you and she are estranged."

"She left my father when I was four," I said. "I did not see her after that, as long as he lived. We had our first meeting yesterday at Ludden Hall in Oxfordshire."

It occurred to me as I spoke that not only would Nelly have doubtlessly disapproved of my talking so

confidentially with a stranger, but that Mr. Harlow
would be most annoyed. A mood of defiance swept
over me. Ultimately this was my affair and I would do
as I liked. I would tell this man who claimed to be my
cousin nothing that he would not find out in the due
course of events.

"And when you spoke to her, she did not tell you
that she had written to me in Canada."

"She made certain implications. Threats. But she
did not mention you by name."

The waiter was hovering over us. I turned my
attention to the soup although I was far from hungry.
When he had been served the salmon, Jason went on.

"It sounds like a very unpleasant situation," he said.
"And I am sorry to be a part of it. Have you any idea
why she should have gone behind your back in this way
and contacted me? She must be determined that you
will not inherit. And you could have done so easily. My
grandfather and my mother are both dead. Neither of
them left any papers which would have given me any
idea of the situation—that property was involved, I
mean."

He was so plausible. If my mother had hired him for
this purpose, if he was a pretender, he was expert.

"She has a great bitterness toward my father," I
said. "They separated under the most unpleasant
circumstances. She would do anything to hurt him,
even now that he is dead."

"But this will not hurt him," Jason argued. "It will
only hurt you."

"She hates me, too," I murmured, and suddenly my
composure shattered. I turned my head away and
pretended to look out the window until the tears dried
in my eyes.

"I think," Jason said carefully, "that it would be well
if both of us considered her state of mind seriously. I
will go to Ludden Hall to talk to her, of course.

Perhaps we could go together."

It was an extraordinary suggestion. But tempting. Unless this was all part of a carefully conceived plan to dupe me, what a revenge it would be on her for me to appear at Ludden Hall with this man—this cousin— who obviously had such sympathy with me.

"Let me put it this way," he went on. "I can understand why she might be bitter, even though I do not know the details. Any separation between husband and wife produces bitterness. But if she had wanted to hurt him, why did she wait until he was dying to contact me?"

He had posed an excellent question. Whatever his true identity, whatever his true motives, it was one which should be answered.

I frowned. "Well, there is this. He allowed her to make Ludden Hall her home as long as he was alive. She has hated the isolation, I gather. But it is a beautiful place. Tudor."

I paused as a wave of memory washed over me. To remember the house was as poignant as to remember the face of a loved one.

"Does it mean that much to you then?"

Why did he have to speak so softly? Why did he have to understand so well?

"Yes," I said simply. "But that is not the point."

"Perhaps it is very much the point."

For a moment we simply looked at one another and I found myself wishing that we had met under other circumstances. But that was folly.

"No," I said. "You asked me why she waited until my father was dying to inform you of your—your heritage."

"My assumed heritage."

"Very well. I think the answer may be that the house was not left to her for life. It is—according to the will— it is mine now. I can ask her to leave and take possession myself. The only qualification is that the house not be sold. But she must have been worried when she learned of my father's illness. She and I are strangers. Whereas my father might have felt some obligation to her...."

"You do not?"

It was a question I had not yet posed. A question I had been avoiding.

"I—I am not clear in my mind concerning my obligations," I said. No matter who this man was, it was impossible, it seemed, to speak less than honestly with him.

"You have no feeling for her?" He shook his head. "No, you must forgive me. I have no right to ask such a question."

"If you are who you say you are," I replied evenly, "you have every right."

His eyes were very intense.

"Do you believe me?" he asked.

This was the point of danger. How could I make myself his ally until I knew the truth?

"No, that is an unfair question, as well," he said. "I'm sorry, Ruth."

"How long will it take to authenticate your certificate of birth?" I said. "Did Mr. Harlow tell you that?"

"Perhaps a week," he replied. "Perhaps less. In the meantime, I think that I, at least, should see your mother. If you will forgive me for saying so, she sounds like a dangerous woman."

"How odd that you should say that, given the circumstances."

"You mean that because of her I have—or may have—an inheritance which I would otherwise have known nothing of?"

"She is your confederate," I said. "Not mine."

He nodded. "That is how it appears," he said. "But

we must consider her motives. It may well be that she has brought me three thousand miles on a fool's errand."

"I don't understand you."

"My mother's marriage certificate may not be valid. According to your mother's letter, your uncle married my mother. But secretly. Perhaps, given the circumstances, the fact that my mother was with child and considering her station, some duplicity may have been exercised. I may very well discover that I have no claims, that before the law I am illegitimate. Your mother may have attempted to use me. And I am not a man who will be used."

The expression in his eyes made it impossible for me to answer. Until now there had been charm. Sympathy. Understanding. I had seen him as a gentle man. But now I saw something else. Something dangerous.

"I'm leaving for Oxford this afternoon," he said, and his voice had a ring of steel to it. "I had intended to wait until my papers had been verified. But now I think that I should talk very seriously to your mother. Her motives for having involved herself seem to be questionable. I find it difficult to believe that a woman would deliberately attempt to strip her own daughter of a fortune."

He looked at me searchingly.

"I have no right even to expect you to trust me," he said in a low voice. "Let alone take my advice. But if I were you, Ruth, I would return to Ludden Hall as soon as possible. It's my opinion that both of us should find out exactly what she wants."

Chapter Five

BY THE TIME I reached the house in Sloan Square I was glad I had delayed my decision. How often my father had warned me not to allow myself to be swept away on a tide of events. And something inside me, some instinct, told me that his advice applied in this case. The thought of appearing at Ludden Hall with Jason as my companion and ally had been too attractive not to be suspect. Besides that, the man's personal charm was too great. I needed to put some distance between us. More than that, I needed to think.

The sun had disappeared behind billowing grey clouds when Williams opened the door and I entered the familiar hall with its black and white marble floor and fluted columns with the sense of having reached a refuge. Giving Williams my cape and feathered hat, I followed the habit of a lifetime and went, as I would have done when troubled in the past, directly to the library.

It was the first time I had entered the familiar room with its ivory colored paneling since the day of my father's funeral. As I drew the sliding double doors behind me and stared at the empty wing chair by the fireplace, I felt a deeper sense of loss than any I had felt since the day my father had slipped away from me. Loss tinged with guilt, for why had I not come here before? All that was left of him was waiting here for me. His beloved books. The busts of Socrates and Ovid. The huge orange and black Etruscan vases.

It came to me as I stood there in the shadows with the leaves of the poplar tree outside beating against the long window by his desk that, without realizing it, I had been avoiding this encounter. That I wished to avoid it still.

Given the normal course of events, surely this would not have been so, I told myself. But from the moment Mr. Harlow had given me the letter and the jewelry box, I had been drawn away from the past and propelled into the future. At first nothing had occupied my mind but the meeting with my mother. And then the wave had begun to roll and take me with it. To Oxford. To Ludden Hall. To Mr. Harlow's office. To Browns Hotel and the meeting with Jason.

And now I had been washed into a familiar backwater. Familiar but strange. For the father I had known had been introduced to me in other forms. Professor Rankin had shown me an impetuous undergraduate, a budding scholar, a sober don. My mother had given me a glimpse of an angry husband bent on revenge. No, more than that. She had given me a nightmare vision of a man who had accepted a heritage that was not his, a man who had murdered his own brother.

Although it was early afternoon still, there was so little light coming through the long windows that it was necessary to light the gas. Once that was done, I seated myself in the leather backed chair behind the desk. Suddenly, as clearly as though my father had spoken to me, I knew what I must do. Too many people had come between us during the past days. I had to try to find him again. How could I make any decision about the future until I had done that?

The top drawer of the desk was open as it always had been and the keys to the other drawers lay inside on a pile of manuscript. Taking the silver chain on which they were strung, I fingered them as my father had so often done when pondering a problem and wondered why I should feel so much the intruder. Surely he must have known that someday I would go through his private papers. His illness had been lengthy and at the beginning he had still been able to come to this room. There had been time for him to destroy anything he had not wanted me to see. And yet I sensed that he had destroyed nothing. In a sense he had given me the symbolic key to the past when he had sent me to Ludden Hall.

The doors slid open silently as I hesitated and Nelly appeared. How was it that I had not noticed until now how pale her face had become? Even her hair seemed more tinged with white.

"Cook has waited lunch for you," she said accusingly.

I realized that I could not tell her that I had lunched already with a man who claimed to be my cousin. She would not understand. It would have to be the first secret between us.

"I'm not hungry," I said awkwardly.

Her eyes narrowed as she saw the keys in my hand.

"I am about to go through my father's papers," I went on in what I hoped was a matter-of-fact voice. "It is time and past that I did so."

I did not ask her to stay and I saw that she recognized the rebuff. Still she persisted.

"You saw Mr. Harlow?"

"Yes."

She waited. Rain began to beat against the windows.

"You want to be alone then?" she said wearily.

I inclined my head, knowing that I was hurting her and yet convinced that there was no other way. This was not the time for confidences. She turned to leave, her shoulders heavy. And then looked back at me.

"Why must you do this today?"

"Today. Tomorrow. What does it matter?"

There was no answer to that question and I think she knew it.

"Are you quite certain you would not like me to stay with you?" she said.

I shook my head.

Again she turned to the door.

"Nelly..." I began.

But there was nothing else to say. The doors closed behind her and she was gone, leaving me alone with only the sound of the rain to break the silence.

Slowly, reluctantly I opened the second drawer and saw a pile of papers covered with the familiar scrawl. His notes for the book on the ruins at Delphi. The book which would never be written now. Unless I.... But this was not the time to think of what I might or might not do.

Another drawer. The gaslight flickered on an album bound in calfskin. Slowly I took it out and placed it on the desk before me. And found my hands were shaking.

If I had hoped to find a record of the past, it was here. Page after page of daguerreotypes, yellowed with age. First a view of Ludden Hall from the hill. Ludden Hall as I had first seen it. The twisted chimney pots. The brick walls clothed with ivy.

I turned the page. Two portraits here. A woman with the thin face of my father. The same sunken eyes, but with a haunted look. Behind her the painted backdrop of a shadowy forest still found in the studios of photographers. And on the page facing her the picture of a man of solid build, his broad chin imprisoned by a stiff, high collar. It was an unfamiliar face except for the mouth, thinly sensual. My father's mouth. I needed no labeling to tell me that this man, this woman, were my grandparents.

Quickly I turned to the next page. Now the man and woman were together and she was holding a baby. The next daguerreotype showed them with two children, one in arms, the other a boy of about eight, leaning against the arm of his mother's chair. The faces of both children were meaningless, unmarked by character.

But the following portraits told their story well. The man who was my grandfather became greyer, broader. The swollen face became increasingly anonymous. But the children took on features all too familiar. The elder son became increasingly like the first portrait of his father with the same thick sweep of dark hair, the same penetrating dark eyes.

Jason's father.

I had no doubt of it.

Breathless, I leafed through the pages until I came to pictures which showed the two boys together. One, my father, must have been fourteen or thereabouts. There was no mistaking the narrow face. The other, already a young man, was the image of Jason. The two brothers stood, arm in arm, smiling at me.

There were no other pictures. The remainder of the album was composed of blank pages.

I felt as though I had followed a path marked for

me, a maze with no direction marked. Replacing the album in its drawer, I unlocked another and found a bundle of letters tied in a faded grey ribbon.

My courage nearly failed me at this point. It was raining harder now and each drop struck the windows like a rebuke. I started to rise to draw the curtains. But my hands seemed to possess a will of their own. The ribbon fell to the floor.

They were love letters, written in an untutored hand. I let my eyes skim the first. A meeting was mentioned. In the arbor. I turned the page. Why was it so difficult to breathe?

Grace.

The name struck out at me.

Grace.

I turned to the last page of the remaining letters. One after another. Letting each one fall to the floor.

Grace.

Jason's mother.

But it had been my father's brother who had loved her. My father's brother who had gotten her with child. My father's brother who had married her. What were these letters doing here?

I knew before I saw the name. There were no headings. The letters began abruptly. But in their context. James. Jamie. Dearest Franklin.

My father's name.

Suddenly the truth overwhelmed me. They had both been her lovers. My uncle and my father. And my uncle had married her. Secretly. Because a child was coming.

Whose child had it been?

If he was my uncle's son, he was my cousin.

Otherwise... otherwise he was my half brother.

I let the remaining letters fall and buried my face in my hands. Two men had loved the same woman. And one had died. And the woman had been sent to Canada.

Oh God!

I heard the doors slide open, heard Williams' voice.

"A gentleman to see you, Miss."

Raising my face from my hands, I saw David standing in the hall.

"I shouldn't have come," he said.

Williams had closed the doors, leaving us alone together.

"No," I said. "I'm glad to see you."

And, in a sense, it was true. I needed to be distracted. The past had closed so tightly about me for a moment that I had been close to suffocating from it. But now, in the presence of a guest, a relative, I had to assume the facade of normality.

"But clearly you're upset."

At least I was not weeping. At the most my face was flushed.

"I've been going through my father's papers," I explained, determined to stay as close to the truth as possible.

"You loved him very much, didn't you?"

David took the wing chair where I had so often curled of an evening and leaned toward me, his hands clasped between his legs. He was neatly dressed in a grey frock coat and striped trousers, but there was none of the elegance about him which Jason had displayed. When we had met in Oxford, he had been wearing evening dress and perhaps that had imbued him with a romance which I no longer saw. He could have been any young scholar down to London for the day.

"Yes, we were very close," I said.

For a moment it seemed as though the conversation had come to an end. I saw him look curiously at the letters strewn about the desk, but I made no explanation. We might be related, in a fashion, and I might have found him sympathetic that evening in Professor Rankin's rooms, but we were really strangers and I would make no confidences. Particularly as I had to presume that he was as fond of his stepmother as I had been of my father. After all, he had asked me to be understanding. I could scarcely tell him how she had betrayed me.

I thought that he would tell me now why he had come. But instead he said: "You must have been disturbed by the—the meeting at Ludden Hall. I blame myself for not having insisted on going with you."

"It was not a particularly pleasant interview," I conceded carefully, "but then I scarcely expected it to be."

Again that silence with only the rain punctuating the moments. How much did he know, I wondered? Had she told him everything? Did he know about Jason and the possibility that I would lose my heritage? Did he know that she was prepared to accuse my father of murder? Because if he knew, he was my enemy.

"Has she told you about our meeting?" I asked when the silence became too strained. It was obvious to me now that he had not come here simply to pay his regards.

"No," he said simply and waited.

"Then may I ask why you are here?" I said, realizing suddenly that I was in no mood to play cat and mouse with him. Although perhaps I was being unfair. Perhaps he was trying to say something and could not find the words. Still, if this had been Jason sitting here, he would have told me. Until that thought came to me, I had not realized how much the meeting over lunch had affected me. Suddenly I was frightened. It was the worst kind of folly to measure every man I met against Jason who might, for all I knew, be a fraud. Whatever

David was, he was not that.

"I'm sorry," I said hastily. "I don't wish to seem ungracious."

"No. Don't apologize." His eyes were troubled. "I came to London on business."

It was an oblique answer. And I mistrusted him for it.

"With me?" I asked coolly.

"No. As a matter of fact, I have come on an errand from my mother."

"She has a message for me?" I asked, not hiding my surprise.

"No. She has no idea that I might come to see you. She sent me to see Mr. Harlow, your solicitor. She has written a letter to him which she did not wish to trust to the post. I have been to his offices already, but he is engaged until four."

"I see," I said. But I did not see. My mind played with possibilities. Jason had spoken of a letter from her, received in Canada. But he had not mentioned a reply. Perhaps he had never made one. If that were so, my mother must be torn with anxiety as to whether her lure had been successful. Perhaps she had written to Mr. Harlow in an attempt to discover if a Jason Bramwell had come to him.

"I know nothing of the contents of the letter," David said suddenly. "Indeed I feel that I have been kept in the dark about a good many things."

"I know the feeling," I said dryly.

"That is why I came here to see you," he went on quickly. The gaslight glittered on his dark hair and carved hollows in his cheeks. He was genuinely troubled. I was sure of that.

I shrugged. "I know nothing," I said. "After what was said between us two nights ago, you must realize that."

"That was before you talked to her at Ludden Hall," David said. "Will you tell me what passed between you?"

I hesitated. I had more reason to trust him than Jason. And yet....

"Why is it important that you know?" I asked him.

Leaning back in the wing chair until his face was in the shadows, he took a deep breath.

"May I ask you some specific questions?" he asked.

"Very well. But I must make my own decision as to whether I will answer them."

I realized that my back was tired. Since he had come into the room I had been sitting bolt upright in the leather chair. And yet I could not relax.

His question, when it came, astonished me. I had expected him to ask what my mother and I had talked about. But instead he said:

"Did you take tea together?"

"Yes," I said, frowning. "As a matter of fact, we did."

"And did my mother—our mother—pour?"

"Yes, of course," I replied, and then, remembering that it was I who had ordered the tea and that it was only with reluctance that she had assumed the role of hostess, I went on.

"Why should such a detail matter to you?"

His hands worked together as though he were molding clay.

"After you left," he told me, "my grandfather returned to the sitting room. From what Mallick tells me, he had been there earlier and was—well, dismissed."

"You said that I would like him," I said inconsequentially. "And I did. He asked me to call him Bertie."

A faint smile brushed David's lips. "He must have been very taken with you then," he said. "But, the point is, he was apparently disturbed at having been barred from your meeting. My—our grandfather is a very curious man."

"It keeps him young."

"Yes." Again that faint smile. "But you can understand that he is a great trial to my mother."

This time he made no attempt to change the "my" to "our." And he was right, of course. She was my mother legally. By blood. But in no important way.

"At all events, he had Mallick bring him back to the sitting room. Apparently they found my mother in a state. According to my grandfather, Mallick poured her another cup of tea. When she drank it, she complained of a certain bitterness."

I stared at him incredulously. What was he trying to say?

"Shortly afterward, having refused to confide in the old man, she excused herself and went upstairs, claiming weariness. Three hours later her maid found her in a stupor on the floor of her bedroom."

"What are you trying to say?" I demanded, starting up from my chair.

"That she was poisoned," David said evenly. "By herself or by someone else. The doctor has been in attendance and it is his opinion that she swallowed a quantity of laudanum."

I caught my breath. The name of the drug was not strange to me. It could be purchased from any apothecary and was useful enough in quieting headaches and in calming children. But everyone knew its dangers. Any derivative of opium could be dangerous. Taken in quantity, it could be deadly.

"She did not come to herself until this morning," David went on steadily. "They had sent for me, of course. I questioned her. So did the doctor. She claims that it was no suicide attempt. She had a bottle of it, of course. Nearly everyone has. But her maid is prepared to testify that there was the same quantity in the bottle as there was a month ago when my mother last had occasion to use it to relieve a pain in her back."

I stared at him incredulously.

"What are you saying?" I demanded. "That I poured a fatal dose in the teapot before I left? That I attempted to murder her?"

Murder.

My mother had been the first to use the word.

"Of course I find it difficult to believe," David said. "No, impossible. And yet the implied accusation was there. If she did not drug herself, then she was drugged. She could have died. And the last thing she drank was the tea. Whenever the dose was administered, the doctor said it would have acted almost immediately. And she had not eaten or drunk a thing until she met you. The servants will swear to that. She was quite coherent, I take it, when you and she talked?"

"Quite coherent," I said in a faltering voice.

"Then, if she is telling the truth—if she did not deliberately poison herself—there was only you and your nurse. . . ."

"Nelly could never have done such a thing," I said breathlessly, at the same time remembering that as we had left, my mother following us into the hall, Nelly had returned to the sitting room for her purse. Could it be that she had put laudanum in the tea? Could she have deliberately come prepared to do something of the sort? Nelly loved me. She had seen me threatened. I remembered the look in her eyes when she had called my mother an evil woman. Involuntarily I began to shiver.

Rising, David came to me and put his hand on my shoulder.

"I have no wish to distress you, Ruth," he said in a low voice, "but you understand that I must know what happened. And, understand this as well. I know that my mother is quite capable of doing anything to have

her way with life. As long as your father was alive, she
had few options. But I have seen the hatred grow. I
know what she is capable of."

"Have the police been notified?" I said stiffly,
moving away from him.

"She wouldn't allow it," David said slowly. "That's
part of what I can't understand. If she really thought
that she had been poisoned, I would have guessed she
would welcome the police. There's so much hatred
inside of her. I may have helped. I reminded her that
you had no reason to wish her harm."

"And of course, I do not," I replied.

Yet at the same moment I spoke, I remembered
Jason. There was an attempt underfoot to disinherit
me. To prove my father a murderer. To cause a
scandal. How better to accomplish everything than to
prove that I had tried to take her life. And yet she had
not allowed the police to be called in.

"There is my grandfather, of course," David was
saying. He was standing deep in the shadows and I
could not see his eyes. "He was in the room when the
last cup of tea was poured."

"And Mallick," I murmured, remembering the
sullen look in the butler's eyes.

"I can think of no reason why Mallick would have
tried to kill her," David said. "As for my grandfather—
well, it is true that they have been at odds ever since I
can remember. When his fortune was finally gone, he
wanted my mother to provide him with funds to
continue his gambling. The craving has never left him.
And, in recent months, there has been a great tension
between them. She wanted to have him put away. She
claims that he is senile."

I shook my head. I knew nothing of Mallick and I
cared little if he were accused of murder. But I did not
want to believe that of the grandfather which David
and I shared between us. No, if anyone had adminis-

tered the laudanum, it must have been my mother herself. She would do anything, doubtlessly, to prove that not only my father but I, as well, would kill to guarantee our fortune.

"What do you believe?" I said quietly.

"I know she nearly died," David told me. "And I know that I love her, whatever her faults may be. I only want to know the truth, Ruth. Believe me. That is all I want to know."

And so we were allies in our way. Both of us wanted to know the truth. And the truth was at Ludden Hall.

"What time do you return to Oxford?" I asked David in a low voice.

"At four. From Paddington."

"I will meet you at the station, then," I told him.

He seemed to understand why I had made my decision. There were no questions.

As soon as David had left the house, I went in search of Nelly.

Chapter Six

IT WAS STILL storming when I reached Paddington at four. Perhaps it was my state of mind which made the glass-domed station seem like a scene from Dante's *Purgatorio*. Gaslight flickered on the white faces of the crowd, turning rushing strangers into anguished souls seeking refuge. The trains, billowing smoke, seemed like huffing monsters waiting for their prey. While Williams saw to the porter, I looked about anxiously for David, and when I saw his familiar face, it was all I could do not to run to him.

He seemed to sense my anxiety, for he took both my gloved hands and held them tight while people pushed past us and whistles shrieked.

"Nelly will follow tomorrow," I said for the sake of nothing more than coming to terms with the commonplace. "I had to tell her what had happened. It was only fair. And she was so upset that I thought it better that she didn't travel tonight."

There was so much noise that I am not certain he heard me, but he smiled, encouragingly. And within minutes we were comfortably settled in a first class compartment with my portmanteau stored on the rack overhead and the train beginning its rocking progress out of the glass cavern.

"I think we can depend on being alone," David told me, removing his top hat and greatcoat and placing them on the seat beside him. "I tipped the conductor well enough, at least."

Rain dashed against the sooty window beyond which the lights of London retreated with remarkable speed. For the first time in hours, I felt myself relax. For a short time, at least, nothing could happen to me. No more shocks. No more alarms. This train, rushing through the darkness, became a sort of sanctuary.

"Do you want to tell me now?" David said. "Or would you like to be quiet for a while?"

He was sitting directly opposite me, so close that our knees nearly touched. The compartment created a sort of intimacy that could never have been found in an ordinary room. In the library at Sloan Square it had been possible to doubt his sympathy, but here I knew that he wanted nothing more than to believe me. His eyes—his demeanor—everything told me so. And so I began.

He listened intently, scarcely seeming to breathe, as I recounted the details of my interview with the woman we both had the right to call our mother. And then, because he asked no questions, I went on to tell him of my meeting with Mr. Harlow that morning.

"A claimant!" he exclaimed when I had finished.

"It's not to be believed. The man must be a scoundrel."

"But I've met him," I said in a low voice. "And I—I believe his story."

It was the first time I had admitted it, even to myself. And, because of the look of incredulity in David's eyes, I knew I had to go on to explain my indiscreet behavior of that afternoon.

"I decided that I must act on impulse," I told him when I had finished describing the luncheon I had shared with Jason. "It's not like me, I admit. My father would not have approved. Neither, I can see, do you. But I had to meet the man and form my own opinion. He wanted me to go down to Ludden Hall with him. Encounter your—our mother together."

"I'm glad you had the wit to refuse that, at least," David said coldly.

He had withdrawn from me in some obscure way. Perhaps it was because he had leaned back in his seat. Perhaps it was because his eyes no longer met mine. His hands were clenched on his knees.

"It's best to know the enemy, surely," I said, with an attempt at levity. I could not afford to lose his sympathy now. I had made him my confidant. My only confidant. He was the only person I could really trust. And he had to realize that. He had to!

"I can't believe that my mother would have written him with such an absurd proposal," David muttered.

"It may be true," I countered. "He has papers. Whether they are valid or not I don't know, but I believe that if they have been falsified, he had nothing to do with it."

"Are you inferring that my mother might have had?"

"Of course not," I retorted, irritated now. "Whatever was done in regard to providing documents concerning Jason's birth was done nearly forty years ago when she was little more than a child. But the point is that she somehow found out about him and took action in a manner which could hurt only one person. Me."

"I won't believe it until I see the actual letter recalling him to England," David said stubbornly.

"Does that mean that you don't believe what I've told you about your mother's implication that my father murdered his brother?" I said defiantly.

"Our mother," David muttered.

"No!" I exclaimed. "From now on I will never refer to her as anything except my father's wife and your stepmother."

He ran one hand over his blond hair, slowly. For a moment, in the dim light, he seemed very young. Scarcely more than a boy. I felt a wave of sympathy. All of this must have come as a great shock to him.

"You have every reason to hate her," he said finally. "But you must not—you *must* not let that warp your judgement, Ruth."

"You love her," I retorted. "And that can warp *your* judgement. Surely you see that. Face the facts. Because they are facts. She wants to prove my father a murderer. She is responsible for Jason having come here to claim the estate my father left me, to deprive me of everything I had every right to think my own. More than that. . . ."

"Yes. Go on."

He was very pale.

"She has done more than that," I went on in a low voice. "It must be obvious to you that she hopes to blackmail me."

"Blackmail?"

It was not the word a lady uses. But I cared little for such details now. A train was speeding through a stormy night. And I was on it through no doing of my own. She had recalled me to Ludden Hall as surely as though she had sent an urgent message. Recalled me to an uncertain future. And he had to realize the degree of her responsibility for everything that had happened since my father's death.

"She has made it appear that someone tried to murder her," I said in an even voice. "When you came to me this afternoon, you were willing to entertain the possibility that I might have put laudanum in that pot of tea, were you not?"

"I told you that I didn't believe that."

"You did. But only because I managed to convince you of my innocence. Nelly, for instance, is still suspect. And your own grandfather. Do you really think that any one of us. . . ."

"I don't know what to think!" David exclaimed. "You're asking me to believe that my mother is some sort of monster. That she'd go so far as to risk her own life to involve you in murder. Her own daughter."

"No!" I cried. "That word implies love. And there is no love between us. None! She wants to destroy me. And my father. Don't you think I realize what sort of position I put myself in in agreeing to return to Ludden Hall? There may be another attempt to 'kill' her. And I'll be on the spot."

I had hoped for so much from this man. He was to be my friend. My confidant. We were not related by blood, but I had been ready to think of him as a brother. And yet I could see from his eyes that his allegiance was to her.

"I was responsible for the police not being called in," he reminded me.

"But you were willing to have me return," I said, "to put myself in the most vulnerable position possible."

"I wanted you to—to come together with her," he told me. "In a real way. You're mother and. . . ."

"Don't say it!" I warned him.

"Why did you return then?"

He had recovered himself. His voice was even,

almost steely. I looked at him and saw a stranger and wished that I had not told him everything. I should have trusted instinct. If I had to return to Oxfordshire, it should have been alone. Or with Jason. The thought of him sparked a sort of longing. I remembered the understanding with which he had greeted everything I said. The idea came to me that he might be on this very train. In a sort of fantasy I saw myself going from compartment to compartment as the train lurched through the darkness, searching for him.

"Why did you agree to return to Ludden Hall?" David repeated. "You say you're placing yourself in some sort of jeopardy."

"I decided to return because I want to talk to her honestly and directly," I told him. "I realize that the safest thing I could do is to promise her that she can remain where she is, that I'll make no attempt to threaten her economic security. I could even promise to—love and cherish her. I don't know if that would be enough. I don't think it would be because I believe she's insatiable."

"Your father taught you how to hate."

I could scarcely hear the words.

"No," I told him. "She taught me. Or perhaps I taught myself because of her. I only know that she means to bring my life down about me like a pack of cards. And I won't let that happen. After you left me this afternoon I decided that it wouldn't be enough to simply stay away from her. My father's death was a signal, you see. A signal for revenge. Whether I stayed in London or not made little difference. She means to destroy me. I know you don't believe that, but it's true. And I won't let it happen. No matter what I have to do."

David made no response. Indeed he did not speak

again until the train reached Oxford. Even then he said only what was strictly necessary, telling me to mind my step as he helped me down onto the nearly deserted platform and asking me if I would like to keep my portmanteau beside me in the hansom cab he hired to take us to Ludden Hall. He answered cautiously enough when I asked him if he would have to return to his college this evening, explaining that he had arranged to stay in the country until, as he put it, his mother had "recovered." He could, he said, go in to his college each day to meet students and deliver lectures.

Since there were so many other things to think about, it was strange that as our carriage rattled through the town, I could do little but regret having seemed so outspoken on the train. It had been foolish of me to suppose that David would abandon the woman who had raised and loved him, even though he was not her real child. We could be friends, David and I, but not confederates. Not in this matter, at least. His side had been chosen for him by his natural affection. I knew that before we reached Ludden Hall I would have to think of some way to make amends. But how to do that without being dishonest, I was not sure.

We had left the storm behind us in London, but there was a light fog and a thin drizzle which did nothing to raise my spirits. I was still sure that I had no choice but to go to Ludden Hall. I had to know what it was that my mother wanted. She had to explain to me why she had sought out Jason, why she was trying in every way she could to harm me. If I could do no more than convince her to talk to me frankly, I would have accomplished something.

To complicate the issue still further, I felt a certain awkwardness about returning to Ludden Hall so soon and without a proper invitation. This time I was making no casual visit, after all. I had some clothes with me and Nelly was to bring more with her

tomorrow. And yet, as far as I knew, no one expected
me, unless David had telegraphed them that afternoon
after I had agreed to come. It was useless to remind
myself that it was, after all, my house. If David had not
withdrawn his friendship, I would have felt more at
ease because, in a sense, I could come as his guest.
Now, as far as I knew, he might abandon me as soon as
we reached Ludden Hall.

To guard against this, if for no other reason, it was
necessary to apologize and I did so with a sincerity
which was real enough. But I could not say I had not
meant what I said.

Now that we were in the country, it was so dark
inside the carriage that I could not see his face, but I
heard him take a deep breath and in a moment his hand
was on my arm.

"I'm sorry, too," he said. "Don't think I can't
understand your point of view. If I didn't know the—
the woman involved, I could sympathize. But I do
know her, and I'm so certain that you're wrong. That
doesn't mean I think your father murdered his brother.
It means that I don't think she ever meant to make that
sort of accusation. She may have wanted to hurt you. I
can see her trying desperately to find some kind of
weapon. I can't excuse that. But she's suffered a great
deal and for a very long time and I'm afraid that I don't
find it as easy to excuse your father's part in it as you
do."

He must have felt me tense because he went on
quickly.

"Let's acknowledge the fact that it's natural for us to
see whatever is going on differently," he said in a long,
urgent voice. "Somewhere there's the truth. I want to
know what it is. And you do, too. Don't you?"

"Of course," I murmured.

And of course I *did*, I told myself. Even if the truth
was something abhorrent to me. Not that it would be,

of course. It was safe enough to speak of truth, if nothing else.

David's hand tightened on my arm. "Then we can work together to discover what the situation really is. I find it difficult to believe that she encouraged this man who claims to be your cousin to come here to England. But I'm willing to agree that it might be part of some sort of revenge. I'm being frank with you, Ruth, because I don't want anything to come between us."

It could have been an awkward moment, but somehow it was not. And almost immediately I was distracted by the lights of the house. They sparkled like diamonds suspended in the night, and although I could not see the hall itself, I could picture it so clearly that tears stung my eyes. And I promised myself that this time I would not leave until everything was settled. It was simply not possible that this lovely manor house was to be snatched away from me so soon after I had discovered it. I would not allow myself even to be disturbed by the possibility. Jason might be sincere, but his claim could not be real. My father would have known the truth. If his brother had truly married the girl, my father would have known. And my father had been an honest man. Scrupulously honest. He would never have taken for himself that which belonged to anyone else, even if that person was an infant. Besides, it was possible that my father had loved Jason's mother. Hopelessly, perhaps, but loved her all the same. I had gathered the letters I had found in the library together after David's visit this afternoon and stuffed them in my portmanteau. Under ordinary circumstances I would never have read them, never have pried into my father's life that far. But now it was necessary that I know all that I could about what had happened forty years ago. Now I had to be completely unscrupulous in order to protect myself and him.

The house loomed up before us now. Lamps hung

on either side of the oak door illuminated the vine covered walls of the first courtyard.

"I have my own keys," David said, jumping to the gravel drive. "No need to disturb Mallick. Here. Keep this umbrella over you while I pay the man here. Now for your portmanteau . . ."

I scarcely heard him. The house seemed to draw me to it. Going to the wall I ran my hand beneath the wet cobweb of ivy and touched the stone itself. Centuries lay there beneath my touch. And it was mine. It must be mine.

The cab was rattling down the drive now, the driver cracking the reins. As though he understood something of the way I felt, David waited by the door until the sound of the carriage and the horses hooves had faded into the misty night. The silence was like velvet. Rich. Voluptuous. The air was fresh and cold. I took a deep breath and followed David into the courtyard, feeling as though the house was welcoming us.

It was a dangerous fantasy and I prided myself on the fact that at least I knew that. I could be dangerously hurt if I allowed myself to want this place too badly, if I let myself love it as though it were alive. Because that was my impulse. To love Ludden Hall in just that way. And it was folly. I stood inside the oak-paneled hall, dimly lit by candles and told myself not to care so much. All of this might be Jason's and not mine.

Somewhere in the depths of the house a clock struck ten and at the same moment, Mallick appeared out of the shadows. In the flickering light, his low-browed face appeared to be expressionless. Perhaps, then, David had telegraphed ahead and I was expected.

David handed him my portmanteau.

"Is my mother still up?" he asked.

"She's in her room, sir. She left word that she wanted to see you as soon as you arrived."

Despite his perfect decorum there was the same

ominous quality about the man that I had noted on my first visit. It was, I thought now, as though he were playing a role. One sensed that his respectful words and bearing had little to do with what was going on in his mind.

"Will you let her know that I am here, then," David said, "and that I will be up to see her in a few minutes? And see that one of the maids prepares the blue room for Miss Bramwell."

"I'm sorry, sir." Was there something mocking in his voice or was it my imagination? "The blue room is already occupied."

"By whom?" David demanded sharply.

"A Mr. Jason Bramwell, sir."

David glanced at me, frowning, and I shook my head. I had had no idea that Jason would put his plan to come here into action so immediately. He must have left London directly after we had lunched together. The knowledge that he was already in this house startled me and I realized that in the back of my mind, at least, I must have counted on confronting the woman who had recalled him to England before he did.

"The green room, then," David said abruptly. "And see that it is prepared immediately. Miss Bramwell is tired."

I realized that I was not to be allowed to see my mother tonight and perhaps it was just as well. If anyone was to talk to her at this late hour it had best be David. Perhaps in the morning he could give me some sort of explanation for her behavior. I did not relish the confrontation which, I knew, had to take place between us, and the more information I had at my disposal the better. Besides, it was true. I was, I found, exhausted emotionally and physically.

"I'll stay with you until your room is ready," David said purposefully, leading the way into the crowded drawing room in which I had been entertained yesterday. I sat in the same chair and accepted the glass of sherry he poured for me. As had been the case in the hall, the only light was from candles.

"So," David said slowly, taking the bellows and blowing the dying fire into life. "We have the added complication of this fellow from Canada to deal with immediately. Perhaps it's just as well. My mother will have to be frank with me about why he is here. Yes, I'll insist that she be frank. I can't be expected to dash back and forth to London carrying messages unless I know what's going on. Especially in light of what you've told me."

I realized then, belatedly, that although I had made him my confidant, he had said nothing about his business with Mr. Harlow that afternoon.

I think I would have asked him had not Mallick made a reappearance, this time carrying a candle. I realized that the house must be completely unequipped with gas. Was that an indication, I wondered, of my father's refusal to spend any money on modernization? Knowing what little I did of my mother I would guess that, given her way, she would have preferred just such a luxury.

"I'm sorry, sir," Mallick was saying, "but your mother requests that you come up to her at once."

David turned to me hesitantly.

"I suppose I should," he said in a low voice. "After all, she was ill yesterday and it is late. Still, if you'd rather not be left alone...."

He glanced around the shadowy room.

"Perhaps you'll remain with Miss Bramwell, Mallick," he went on.

It was all I could do to keep myself from shuddering. This house had no fears for me but I had no desire to be alone with Mallick.

"No," I said a little too loudly. "I'll be quite all right.

Go along upstairs, by all means. I'll see you in the morning."

There was a strangely anxious look in David's eyes as he took his leave and I wondered if, despite his assurance that he would insist on his mother's frankness, he dreaded the interview.

Silence descended as soon as he and Mallick had left the room and the door was shut behind them, a silence so deep and penetrating that a scream rose in my throat when I heard the sound of something moving behind me.

"Perhaps you'll help me over to the fire, gel," my grandfather said. "You were long enough in getting here."

With my hand clasped firmly over my mouth, I looked behind me and saw the scarecrow figure of the old man leaning heavily on a cane.

"Frightened you, didn't I?" he chortled. "Always liked surprises, I did, even as a boy. There I was sitting in that sofa there in the corner, neat as you please, and none of you guessed a thing. Not that Mallick might not have noticed me and said nothing. It's the man's way. Come along with you, gel!"

I went to help him, too startled to speak, and he leaned against me as light as hollow bones until I lowered him into a wing chair by the fire.

"That's right, gel. Back to the door. Anyone comes poking in, you pretend you're by yourself. Get rid of them. You're the type knows how to do that sort of thing. That's why I waited up for you. Took a bit of doing, but the lad who wheels my chair and tucks me in and such is fond of the odd shilling, don't you know?"

"So you knew I was coming," I said in a low voice. It was strange how guilty I felt. And for no reason except that I knew that the old man should be in bed. But then, why should he, I asked myself defiantly. He was not a child, and despite what my mother had said, I did not think him senile. It was only a bit after ten and not the wee hours of the morning. Still, despite my attempt at self assurance, I knew that I would find the situation extremely awkward if someone were to find us together.

"Up in her room I was when the wire came," my grandfather informed me in a creaking voice, nodding his white head from side to side. He was, I noted, wearing evening dress of the same ancient vintage of the frock coat worn the afternoon before. In spite of the shabbiness of his clothing, however, it was easy to see something of the man-about-town he once had been. It was there in the knowing expression in his eyes and the languid manner in which he crossed his legs, displaying well polished evening slippers.

"She wasn't angry. That's the thing that I don't understand," he mused, his eyes fastened on the untouched glass of sherry I was holding.

Although we knew each other very slightly, my grandfather and I, there were levels at which we communicated with the accomplishment usually developed by long proximity. I smiled and handed him the glass.

"Thank 'e, gel," he said, accepting the sherry with good grace. "Did I tell you to call me Bertie, gel?"

In spite of my desire to remain as quiet as possible, I broke into laughter which I attempted to muffle by pressing my hands against my lips. It was clear from the expression in my grandfather's pale, blue eyes that he shared my amusement. No doubt my mother would use his desire to have me call him by his given name as a sign of dotage on his part, but I knew that, on the contrary, he was simply marking the outlines of a more subtle and rather delightful relationship between us. It was clear that he liked me. I wondered if he had risked his daughter's anger in order to give me information I ought to have before seeing her, or for purposes of his own.

"Pleased enough she was that you were coming back with Davie," my grandfather went on, smacking his lips over the sherry. "Now, soon as I saw that, I said to myself, 'The gel's got something to worry about and that's the truth.'"

I knew that he was referring to me, and I could understand his concern. Indeed, I shared it. If my mother had been pleased to hear that I was coming to Ludden Hall, it must mean that such a visit suited her purposes. And since I knew enough about her to be certain that she wanted nothing better than to hurt me, it was clear that I was here at my own risk.

"I came because David told me that an attempt had been made on her life," I said.

"What's that?" The old gentleman cocked his shaggy white eyebrows at me. "What's that you're saying, gel?"

A chill seemed to drop over me, engulfing me like an icy blanket. Was my grandfather saying that there had been no overdose of laudanum? But if that were true— if that were true . . . David could not have lied to me! I refused to believe it. Why should he have told me such a thing if it wasn't true? What purpose would it serve? What purpose had it served? To lure me here to this house? That was the answer. But the old man had to be mistaken. Perhaps my mother was right. Perhaps he *was* losing his grip on his mind . . .

"I was told," I said steadily, "that she was found ill in her room last night, after my nurse and I had left."

"Vapors! That's what I told the doctor. Ladies always get their own way with vapors. Why I remember old Bellinger's daughter, Lady Frances. . . ."

"Then she *was* ill!" I exclaimed, weak with relief.

How important it had been that there be no suspicion that David had lied to me.

"She was always a trickster," my grandfather said thoughtfully.

For a moment I was not certain whether he meant the recollected Lady Frances or my mother. His eyes were veiled now, as though he had retreated into the past, but just what past I was not sure.

"Tried to wind me 'round her finger soon as she could talk," he continued and I realized that he was speaking to the point again. I wondered just how much he knew about the overdose of laudanum and whether or not I could coax him into telling me what he knew. Or perhaps I would not have to coax but only wait until he was ready. Still I hoped that he would not prolong his reminiscences overlong and risk an interruption.

"Clever with her tongue, she was," the old man went on thoughtfully. "Took after me in that. Lie like a trouper when it suited her. But I was a match for her. Until the money was gone. Unfair game now that she holds all the cards."

One bony finger touched his eyes as though he were wiping tears away and I felt a flood of compassion for him. I had not forgotten the way my mother had spoken to him yesterday when she had found him with me in this room. I had had the sense then that he was little more than a prisoner in this house, that there was little love between them. And I remembered, too, that David had said that his grandfather had returned here after I had left. If laudanum had been poured in the teapot, he might have had the chance to do it and the reason, as well.

"Did she lie about being poisoned?" I said in a low voice. Better to come directly to the point whether he wished to or not.

"Take it serious, don't you, gel?"

He did not seem particularly surprised, or even

interested. We might have been discussing the weather.

"David told me," I said. "That's why I came back. I understand that she made certain accusations."

I waited. My grandfather seemed to shrink back into the wing chair. The glass of sherry shook precariously.

"It's what she wanted," the old man said. "To have you back here. London's too far."

I was not sure what he meant by that, but rather than find out I decided to stick to the subject of poison.

"Do you think she took the laudanum herself?" I asked him. "Or did someone really try to murder her?"

"She's a dangerous woman."

I sighed. Either he did not know any more than I did or he was determined not to tell what he did know directly.

"Is she capable of having given herself an overdose?" I pressed him. "Would she have taken that chance. . . ."

"There's damn little that woman wouldn't do to get what she wants, gel. But I think you're a match for her. That's why I waited up to talk to you. That's why. . . ."

I shook my head to warn him as Mallick appeared in the doorway. He had come on us so silently that I had no way of knowing how long it had been since he had opened the door, no way of knowing how much he had heard. The wing chair my grandfather was sitting in had its back to the man, but he must have heard my grandfather's last words, at least. He must have realized that I was talking to someone. And yet he gave no sign. His dark, blunt featured face was as expressionless as ever.

"Your bedroom is ready, Miss," he said.

My grandfather sat motionless. Even the glass of sherry was steady now.

"Thank you, Mallick," I said. "If you will give me directions I will go up myself when I'm ready."

He hesitated and I guessed that he, too, was remembering my mother's rage when she had discovered, yesterday afternoon, that her orders had been disobeyed, that the old man had not been kept out of the way.

"It may be difficult for you to find your way, Miss," Mallick said. There was a challenge in his voice.

"I expect I can manage," I replied and saw my grandfather grin in the shadows of the wing chair.

"Very well, Miss." He might as well have been telling me that I took the responsibility of my *tête à tête* on my own shoulders. "There's a staircase to the right of the corridor. The green room is the fifth on the right just beyond where the upstairs hall turns left. You can take one of these candles."

With that he disappeared, closing the door behind him. The perfect butler, if that was what he was.

"Don't trust the man," my grandfather muttered. "He's a rascal. Tells *her* everything."

It was odd, I thought, that so far neither of us had referred to *her* as either daughter or mother. It was as though both of us were reluctant to acknowledge the relationship. There was reason enough for me, of course, but his feeling for her had to be deeper, even though age had brought natural resentments.

I had hoped that we could return to the subject of the laudanum, but my grandfather continued to rail against Mallick.

"Came with the house, he did," the old man muttered. "But there's no telling anything else about the fellow. Wouldn't be surprised if he'd seen the inside of a gaol in his time. Low forehead like that always tells. Warned her to get rid of him, I did, right at the start. But she wouldn't listen. Wasn't long before they were as thick as thieves, the two of them. Not in the ordinary way. Could have understood that, her stuck away here without a man. There now, I didn't mean to shock you, gel. Out of the habit of talking to young ladies."

I was torn between amusement and impatience.

"Something's up," my grandfather said in a conspiratorial manner, placing one finger beside his nose and, in so doing, managing to spill what little was left of the sherry on the arm of the chair.

"There's this foreigner to consider," he went on in a penetrating whisper as I dabbed at the stain with my handkerchief.

It took me a minute to realize that he meant Jason.

"You've met him?" I demanded.

My grandfather shook his head regretfully. "But the boy told me he was from Canada. Name of Bramwell. Relative of yours?"

His faded eyes brightened with curiosity, and I realized that I would have to tell him what I knew. Tomorrow, though. There was no time tonight to go through the explanation I had already made to David, particularly since it was doubtful that he could tell me anything I did not already know. After all, he had never known my uncle. His connection with my father's family had begun, like my mother's, long after Jason's birth.

And yet my mother had known enough about events which had taken place years before she had met and married my father to cause the present troubled situation. It might be that my grandfather could give me some clue.

But already his mind had strayed from the presence of a stranger in the house.

"You and I, gel," he said, leaning forward until the candlelight streaked his white hair with gold. "You and I must stick together. I'll tell you this. She'll do you a bad turn if she can. And she's a clever bitch, no doubt about it, though I say so who shouldn't. She wants me out of the way, you see."

His voice broke and I could see something like fear in his eyes. I knew that he was about to tell me whatever it was that had kept him waiting here for me in this shadowy room.

"She says I've lost my wits," he told me. "Gone dotty. Wants to put me in an asylum. And all because I know more than it suits her for me to know."

His claw-like hand reached out for me and I took it.

"You won't let her do it, will you, gel?" he whispered plaintively. "I'm an old man, but you're young and strong. You'll protect me, won't you, gel?"

Not since my father's death had I felt such tenderness for anyone. No, more than tenderness. Compassion, mingled with determination. I had had no choice but to let my father slip away from me. Death had been an enemy I could not fight in the end. But I could keep this old man safe. And I would do it.

"No need to fear," I said, unconsciously adopting his idiom. "I'll take care of you no matter what happens."

This time I heard the door open, but it was not Mallick returning as I first thought. David crossed the room in long strides and stared down at his grandfather.

"Davie, lad," the old man said with what seemed to me to be a hypocritical show of affection.

David glanced at me accusingly.

"He was waiting," I said in a low voice. "He wanted to talk to me."

Although he did not say that he could not believe that the old man and I had anything to say to one another, David clearly believed that to be the case. He shook his head.

"I'll help him to his room," he said in an icy voice. "If you'll wait here, I'll return shortly and show you to yours. It's nearly midnight."

His attitude annoyed me. Furthermore it was clear that whatever had passed between him and his mother, he did not intend to share with me. At least not tonight.

"Mallick gave me directions," I said shortly. "I'll find my own way."

"You won't forget what I said, gel," my grandfather mumbled as I rose.

Impulsively I leaned down and kissed his forehead.

"I won't forget," I murmured. "Goodnight."

"Bertie."

He said it with such a show of buoyancy that my heart went out to him.

"Bertie," I repeated, smiling.

David frowned, but I paid no attention to him, briskly leaving the room after pausing to pick up a candlestick. My annoyance had turned to anger. He had been friendly enough when he had wanted to find out about Jason, but now it was amply clear that he did not intend to share information with me. Very well, then. I was perfectly capable of dealing with the complexity of family affairs myself. And if I were to discover tomorrow that he sided with his mother in her intention to exile my grandfather to an asylum, he would discover that I could be a formidable opponent. After all, until it was proved otherwise, this house and everything in it belonged to me.

My bravado deserted me as soon as I left the sitting room, however. It was not the house, I told myself, as I groped my way along the corridor to the stairs. If I had been alone here, my heart would not have pounded like this. There was nothing malignant about Ludden Hall. Only the people in it.

The stairs seemed endless, turning first to the right and then the left. Every step creaked. The very darkness seemed murky as though it possessed a substance of its own. I tried to calm myself by repeating

Mallick's directions to myself. My room was fifth on the right just where the corridor turned left. But now, standing at the top of the stairs with only the candle's wavering glow to guide me, I realized that the corridor ran in both directions.

For a moment I felt a sense of panic. No use to return to the sitting room. David would already have left it with the old man in tow, probably to a bedroom on the first story, since it seemed doubtful that my grandfather could mount stairs, even with assistance.

Desperately I tried to picture the outside of the house to give myself some sense of direction. Were I to turn right I would be in one of the wings which embraced the courtyard and, in that case, the corridor would not turn left since that wing terminated in the gatehouse.

Very well, then, I would go to the left. Holding my candle high in front of me I saw that there must be another interior courtyard, for to my left there were mullioned windows beyond which the night pressed like a dark blanket. Carefully I counted the doors to my right. One. Two. Three. Four. All closed forbiddingly. And then the corridor turned to the left. I took a deep breath of relief. The first door on my right would be the one to my room, of course. How absurd of me to have been frightened.

Grasping the knob confidently, I turned it and found myself in a large chamber lighted by what seemed to be hundreds of candles which blazed from sconces on the wall and from the tops of tables. For a moment the glare blinded me. And then I saw my mother reclining against a mountain of pillows on a bed canopied with red velvet hangings.

"An unexpected pleasure," she said in a voice which gave a lie to her words.

For a woman who had nearly died of laudanum poisoning little more than twenty-four hours before, she looked remarkably well. Her red hair was caught high on her head and fell in ringlets about her face and the pink nightgown she was wearing showed beautifully molded shoulders. She might have been waiting for a lover for her color was high, although her eyes were dull. For all my shock at seeing her, it occurred to me that she might have been expecting me and I wondered if Mallick had given me incorrect directions deliberately.

But no, that could not have been. For all he had known, I might have agreed to accompany him upstairs, and then he would have had no recourse but to show me my own bedroom. Seeing me must have surprised her as much as I was to find myself here, and yet she did not seem to be displeased.

"How gracious of you to stop by to say goodnight," she said with the same veiled irony. "You must excuse me for not having been downstairs to welcome you, but as you must know, I have been—ill."

Hating myself for my own awkwardness, I began to explain that I had had no intention of disturbing her and that I was merely searching for my room.

"Never mind," she interrupted. "Now that you are here, we must have a little talk. Mothers and daughters do have midnight talks, I understand."

It was a challenge I could not put off with pleas of weariness. Indeed, I had never felt less like sleeping. All the outrage I had felt about the turn of events which had caused me to return to Ludden Hall engulfed me, and I nodded as I closed the door quietly behind me and went to stand beside the bed.

Perhaps the willingness with which I responded to her invitation disconcerted her, for her laughter was shrill.

"Do put out your candle, my dear," she said. "As you can see there is quite enough illumination."

I did as she told me, feeling, as I did so, the full

extent of my disadvantage. The furnishings of the room alone were enough to induce a sense of claustrophobia for every inch of the carpeted floor seemed to be covered with tables hidden under fringed clothes, with horsehair sofas and chairs, and even, in the corner, a rosewood spinet. Every available surface was covered with objects: glass vases cupped clumps of dried flowers and wax fruit; pictures stood in silver frames; and there were silk plumes rising from gilt vases. The walls were covered with scarlet and gold paper of an intricate design and the long windows were hidden behind red velvet drapes. It was as though the mania for objects that had been apparent in the sitting room downstairs had been allowed to run riot here.

"I expect you find my taste quite appalling," I heard her say. "Your father must have taught you to appreciate simplicity. It was a great misfortune, I often thought, that he was not born an ancient Greek."

"It's an interesting room," I said, sitting down in a little chair upholstered in green plush.

"I suppose you think it gives you an insight into the extent of my vulgarity," my mother responded. "Just as the jewelry must have done. I've often imagined the utter dismay with which your father would have looked at this room. You have that exact look in your eyes now. I can't express the pleasure it gives me to see you look that way. Even the ceiling is a triumph, don't you think?"

Looking up I saw that it had been painted amber, the gloss so high that it almost created a mirror effect. I seemed to see the shadow of myself, and quickly averted my eyes.

"But of course you have little interest in discussing my abilities as decorator," my mother said. "I have talked to David and I know that you are considerably disturbed, as, of course, you should be."

"Curious would be the better word," I replied tartly.

"I, too, have talked to David and I understand that you believe that either Nelly or I might have been responsible for your—your illness, as you put it."

"What I believe is neither here nor there," she said and there was no longer any irony in her voice. "I nearly died. That much is fact. As to who is responsible, I have made no charges."

"But you have been busy in other ways," I reminded her. "It was on your account, I believe, that Jason Bramwell—if that is indeed his name—was brought to England."

"An agreeable gentleman, don't you think? How clever it was of you to arrange a meeting with him. I must confess I was surprised by your initiative. Your father would never have acted so—may I say, impulsively. But, of course, you were very clever. Jason was most impressed with you. And sympathetic. Yes, he is very sympathetic. Even so I am sure that he will press his claim. We had such an interesting talk, he and I, and I was able to make him understand that he should not let his compassion for your situation stand in his way. Justice must be done, of course."

For a moment I stared at her, uncertain of how to respond. She was being disconcertingly direct. I had expected her to deny her involvement, but apparently she was willing to admit to what she had done quite openly.

"You must hate me very much," I said, and then cursed myself for that was not at all what I had intended to say.

"I have only hated one person in my entire life," she said in a low voice, "and he is dead."

"That does not make him helpless," I replied.

"By that you mean, I suppose, that you will act as his champion," she said scornfully.

"If the man who claims to be my cousin is not that," I said, "if he is someone you have paid to play a part, I will charge you both with criminal collusion."

"I believe you would," she said softly. "You have something of my spirit, Ruth. You must be careful or I may end by loving you."

I had thought that nothing she could say could hurt me. But it was as though, with a single word, she had wounded me past all endurance. How could she speak of love? How could she?

I would not let her see the tears which had risen, quite unbidden, to my eyes. And if she were not to see them there was nothing but retreat open to me.

Blindly I groped for one of the many candlesticks and rushed to the door. And heard her laugh softly.

"The next room is yours, my dear," I heard her say. "Sleep well. Sleep well."

Chapter Seven

SUNLIGHT, FILTERED THROUGH the faded damask curtains, woke me. The night before I had been too exhausted to do more than note with thankfulness that I had been given a room which my mother had not marred with bric-a-brac, and now in the dim golden light I realized with delight that the furnishings matched the antiquity of the house. A vast oak chest, the wood mellowed with age, stood in one corner of the spacious chamber and a high oak cabinet scrolled with carvings was situated against the wall facing the bed. Pushing myself up against the bolster, I saw that the carpet, although faded and worn, was elegantly patterned. The hangings on the high postered bed were of the same yellow and green damask as the draperies which covered four long windows.

Pushing the coverings aside, I jumped from the high bed as eagerly as though I were a child again and hurried to a window. There was no fire burning in the fireplace and the air was cold and dank, but as soon as I had drawn the musty drapes aside and thrust the casement window open, I smelled the fresh, crisp breeze of an autumn morning. Below me lay a courtyard, larger than the one through which I had passed the night before, a courtyard of graveled paths and untended beds of late roses. Yew hedges marked the outlines of what had once been a formal garden. And about it all ran the mellow brick of the house itself like a sheltering arm, the stone mullioned windows glistening in the sunlight.

A great yearning filled me. It was all so lovely. How could I bear to let it go? And yet I had to face the fact that all this beauty might belong to someone else.

I think that was the first moment in which I truly considered my position. My heart sank as I realized that it was not simply a matter of possibly losing Ludden Hall, although that was the most important thing. If Jason was who he said he was, if his claim were valid, not only would all this slip through my fingers, but I would lose my independence as well. Everything my father had left me would be his and I would be left with nothing. Although I had never known poverty, I had seen it often enough in the streets of London. Since I had first set eyes on Ludden Hall I had not given another thought to the possibility of finding employment at the British Museum. But now that, or a post as governess in someone else's house might be my future.

I think I could have faced it better if I had never come here. The house in Sloan Square had been my home all my life and there were fond memories attached to it. But never would it have hurt me to leave

those familiar rooms as deeply as it would to realize
that never again could I kneel in the deep embrasure of
this window and look down into an unkempt garden
which seemed so strangely familiar.

I was distracted from my misery by a tapping at the
door. A flushed faced maid came hesitantly into the
room carrying a copper can full of hot water.

"I'm Rose, Miss," she said, averting her eyes,
whether from shyness or the unexpected sight of seeing
me kneeling by the window clad only in my nightgown
I do not know.

Rising, I took my robe from the bed, hoping that
there was no sign of tears in my eyes.

"Is it very late, Rose?" I asked her. "Is your mistress
down to breakfast yet?"

"Oh, the mistress never comes downstairs before
twelve, Miss, and it's only nine now."

Expertly she tipped the copper can over the
flowered china basin which was set on a small oak
stand near the door.

"Perhaps you'd like a tray in your room, too, Miss,"
she went on, more boldly now.

"No, I'll go downstairs. Has Mr. Bramwell
breakfasted yet?"

"Oh, yes, Miss, and Mr. David, too."

Apparently gratified by my questions, she began to
beam and set the copper pot down as though she was
prepared to stay and talk indefinitely. It occurred to me
that later it might be a good idea to involve her in a
prolonged conversation. There were a good many
things about my mother's household that I could learn,
and I was prepared to be as unscrupulous as necessary
in order to prepare myself for the battle which had
already begun between us.

"Mr. David was off early to Oxford," Rose
contributed voluntarily. "He said he'd be back this
afternoon. And Mr. Bramwell just now finished and

went out for a walk about."

I allowed her to prattle on as she busied herself unpacking my portmanteau, although she said little of interest. A local girl, she was primarily concerned with village affairs and I found myself envying her as she spoke of her father, busy now with the harvest, and of the young man she intended to marry. It was clear that no one had taken pains to train her in the discretions of her position and she seemed to take it for granted that I would be as interested in her chatter as though I were one of her friends.

"Oh, Miss, you're in mourning!"

Having finished my toilet, I had slipped on the plain black muslin gown I had worn the day before. It was a simple frock, decorated only with a bit of black lace about the neck and the cuffs of the fitted sleeves, and with three flounces on the skirt which hung in loose folds without the benefit of a crinollette—an article of clothing which I despised.

"My father died recently," I replied, fastening the jet buttons of the bodice, and wondering as I did so whether this girl had any real knowledge of who I was or of the fact that my father's death had also meant the death of her mistress' husband.

"I'm that sorry, Miss," she murmured and I saw that her face was flushed again as though she were embarrassed. "Here I have been chatting away and that after Mr. Mallick warned all of us the way he did."

She had closed the empty portmanteau and was out of the room before I could ask her what she meant. Had Mallick been given directions to warn the servants not to answer any questions that I might put to them? I thought it only too likely and promised myself I would not let such manoeuvring stand in my way. I had come here to discover the truth about the past and to prove to my mother that she could not hurt me, and that was what I intended to do. I glanced in the mirror, an

ancient bit of glass which curved my features, and saw
her in the reflection. I remembered what she had said
the night before about not letting herself love me and
lost my bravado in an instant. For she had already hurt
me.

I breakfasted by myself in a sunny breakfast room
which, like my bedroom, was unadorned by my
mother's touch. The walls were paneled with warm oak
and the table, chairs and buffet were of the same wood.
With the sun streaming in through the thick, diamond-
shaped panes of glass, I felt as though I were in a warm,
brown nest as I sipped the tea which had been brought
to me by a girl who looked enough like Rose to be her
sister.

My mood shifted as rapidly as the shadows which
came and went as clouds raced across the sun. One
moment I would feel completely content and utterly
safe as I let the mood of the house engulf me. The next
minute the sense of yearning I had felt earlier in my
bedroom would take possession of me and I would feel
as though I must weep. I realized, as I set the blue and
white Spode cup in its saucer, that I had to determine
my position in regard to Ludden Hall as quickly as
possible. There could be no games of cat and mouse. It
was up to Jason to make the necessary moves and I had
to see that he made them promptly. The attempt on my
mother's life—if there really had been an attempt—her
determination to destroy my father's reputation were
matters which I could not deal with until I knew my
position.

Remembering that Rose had said that Jason was
outside, I went to find him, first in the smaller
courtyard at the front of the house and then outside the
walls. Despite the sun, the air was brisk and I shivered,
knowing that I should have gone upstairs to get my
pelisse, but was too intent on my search to return to the
house. The sheep still grazed the lawns, but now they

were at the east side of the house where a line of high,
ragged yew hedges bordered the beginning of the hill.
As I bent to run my hand along the thick wooly back of
one of the animals, someone called my name.

It was Jason. I realized, as he came striding toward
me, that there was something about his dark face that I
had not remembered, a certain withdrawn quality. It
gave him, at a distance, the air of a perfectly dressed
stranger in one of the new tweed suits which were just
now becoming the vogue for country wear and a grey
derby which hid his thick hair. It was only when he was
close to me, his hat removed and his eyes intent on
mine, that I remembered the extraordinary power of
the man to make me feel an intimacy between us that
did not exist.

"But I had no idea you were here!" he began.

I began to explain that I had arrived late the night
before, but the wind caught the skirts of my gown,
whirling them about so that I was forced to turn my
entire attention to controlling them.

"Here. Come with me," Jason said, offering me his
arm, and in a minute we were in a small summer house
of the sort called a gazebo. Such a modern touch had to
be, I knew, due to my mother's efforts. How absurd,
with such delightful courtyards to catch the sun, to
have erected this flimsy, wicker structure outside the
walls simply because it was fashionable. It was indeed a
fortunate thing, I thought, that lack of money had
prevented her from making Ludden Hall some sort of
monstrous showplace for the latest modes.

"I'm glad you're here," Jason said, sitting down
beside me on one of the benches which lined the walls.
"I came down here directly after we talked yesterday
because I knew that this affair couldn't be left in limbo.
It wouldn't be fair to you."

Once again he had spoken directly to the point and I
felt myself warming to him as I had the day before.

"I intended to stay in Oxford and restrict myself to

calling on your mother, but she was insistent that I stay here. No one could have been more cordial."

"It's a side of her I haven't had the pleasure of seeing," I said dryly.

"No, I expect you haven't," he replied sympathetically. "It's as you said. She's a very bitter woman. But I think you're mistaken about one thing. She hates your father, but she doesn't hate you."

"That's rather beside the point, isn't it," I retorted.

"Perhaps. I only thought that if you could see her in another light."

"Did she tell you that she suspects me of having attempted to poison her the day I came here?" I asked.

"Good lord, no!"

As quickly as I could, I explained about the laudanum, and how David had come to London to tell me about it.

"That's why I'm here," I concluded. "I realized that I had to defend myself."

"Perhaps, under the circumstances, you would have done better to have stayed away," Jason said in a low voice, his face thoughtful. "I wouldn't have urged you to come if I had realized that she could be that vindictive."

"So you think she took the overdose deliberately?"

He shrugged. "How can I tell? I didn't talk long with her. That was the reason she gave for wanting me to stay. She said that she had been ill and that she would feel stronger today. That was one of the reasons I didn't press her as much as I wanted to."

I remembered the behavior of the woman in whose bedroom I had sat the night before and thought that she had indeed made a remarkable recovery for someone who had so lately been the near victim of a poisoning attempt.

"But you did ask her why she wrote to you," I murmured.

Jason laughed harshly. "Oh, she made no secret of

the reason for that. She was brutally honest about wanting to revenge herself. I only wonder why she waited so long."

"I expect I know the answer to that," I told him. "My father kept certain—evidence which would have permitted him to divorce her."

"Then the revenge was not all on her part," Jason said in a low voice, and then grew silent. It struck me how strange it was that when I was with him I could talk as though his claim to the estate had already been proved valid.

"She was stubborn on one other point," Jason said slowly. "When I asked her how she came to find out about my existence, she refused to tell me."

I clenched my hands. This was exactly the sort of thing he would tell me if he and my mother had contrived this plan between them. And, ironically enough, that was not how I wanted to see him, as a criminal conspirator. His next words came almost as a relief.

"I must find some way to force her to tell me," he muttered, almost as though he were speaking to himself. "But it will be difficult. Particularly if the documents I brought with me are valid. I put them in the hands of your solicitor before I left London and he is having a check made at Somerset House. We should know in a few days. Perhaps tomorrow."

I stared at him, puzzled. Something in what he had just said did not make sense.

"You see, Ruth," he went on, "she says that she has a witness who will swear that he or she actually saw my father being murdered."

My head spun.

"But that can't be true," I cried. "Mr. Harlow told me that your father—that my uncle drowned. My father tried to save him."

I broke off and clasped my hands to my mouth.

"Yes," Jason said as he saw understanding dawn in my eyes. "I'm sorry, Ruth, but that is what she intends to claim. Unless. . . ."

"Go on." My mouth was so dry that I could scarcely speak. "Unless what?"

"She says she will remain quiet if I accept the estate. It's a form of blackmail. I'm to provide her with what she referred to as 'ample funds,' and she will set herself up in London. Re-enter society. She was quite businesslike about it. It must have been an ace card that she decided to use when she discovered that I found the idea of taking this house and all the rest away from you distasteful. She's a very clever woman, Ruth, and quite clearly very dangerous as well."

It was such a bizarre story that at first I could not comprehend it. Gently and clearly Jason repeated it. If he did not, for whatever reason, take possession of the estate, part of which he must agree to share with her, she would make the charge of murder public. It was the sort of news that the penny tabloids liked to print. Closing my eyes, I could see the headlines. DEAD MAN NAMED MURDERER. WELL-KNOWN ANTIQUARIAN KILLED BROTHER.

"It isn't true!" I burst out. "If you had known him, you'd be as sure as I am that it isn't true!"

Rising, I stumbled to the door of the gazebo. Instantly Jason was beside me, his hand on my elbow.

"Do you want to walk for a while?" he asked me.

There was something different about his voice, a certain tightness. I looked up at him and found that the expression in his eyes had changed as well. Was he thinking, perhaps, of the man he had never known, the man who was his father? I saw him glance at the house and wondered if he was thinking of all the years he had been deprived of his heritage. If this nightmare story of my mother's was true, he had every right to hate me, or at least to hate my father.

But when he spoke, I discovered that his anger was directed toward my mother.

"I am not the sort of man to be manipulated," he said in an even voice. "I've had a night to think about this. I can't be sure what to do, but one thing I know. Under no circumstances will I allow her to make this wild story of hers public."

"Do you think it's a complete fabrication?" I asked him.

We were walking along the graveled path which led to the back of the building. Here the gentle hills rose on three sides of the house and sloped like green velvet to a meandering river that ran through a meadow below the grass terrace on which we found ourselves. For a moment we stood silent and I knew that both of us shared a mental image of a young man struggling in the water, and another forcing him below the surface. Taking a deep breath which was almost a gasp, I swept the picture out of my mind.

"Do you really believe there could be any truth in it?" Jason asked me. Coming to stand between me and the river, he put his hands on my arms and looked at me with dark-eyed intensity.

"No," I told him evenly. "My father wasn't the sort of man who could ever have killed anyone, let alone his own brother."

But even as I said the words I was remembering scraps of what Professor Rankin had told me. When he had first met my father they had both been wild young men. I remembered thinking at the time that he was describing a man I had never known. And there was the matter of my father's strange attitude toward this house. Why had he stayed so far from it? Because of a tragedy, Professor Rankin had said. Could it be that the tragedy was murder? They had loved the same girl,

Jason's mother. And Harry had gotten her with child. Had the knowledge of that enraged the younger brother?

Jason was saying something to me, but I could not take in the words. If someone had indeed told my mother this story, if it were not simply a fabrication, then that person might know that my father had had reason to want his brother dead. For the first time since I had left London the day before, I remembered the letters I had hastily stuffed in my portmanteau. Letters my father had received from Grace Evans! Surely they would tell me something. When I had first discovered them, I had wondered if I had any right to read them, but now I knew I had to.

"Are you listening to me, Ruth?" I heard Jason say. His hands were still tight on my arms.

"I'm sorry," I said slowly, my eyes focusing on him as though I were awakening from a trance. "Something occurred to me."

"Something that I should know?"

Whatever power it was that he had over me was so great that I nearly told him about the letters then and there. But I stopped myself in time. Why was it so difficult for me to remind myself that for all I knew this man might have plotted all this with my mother? He and she between them might have....

"No," I said aloud, but my mind was on another course entirely. If I could simply approach this from the premise that no matter how sincere Jason seemed, he was not the heir, then everything would seem quite different. Pulling myself away from Jason I went to stand by the low stone wall which divided the terrace from the water meadow. Staring down at the twisting river, I forced myself to concentrate. An idea was lurking in the corner of my mind and something was keeping me from grasping it.

And then, quite suddenly, I knew what it was. If

Jason was not who he claimed to be, the great difficulty
was the forged documents. He and my mother might
have been clever enough to have had the marriage and
birth certificates made up. I had no doubt that such a
thing was possible. But probably they would want to
avoid any sort of legal battle in which the authenticity
of those papers would be checked with great care.

The stone of the wall was warm under my hands. I
shut my eyes to help myself concentrate. Because it all
came back to me. The success of their plan depended
on my reaction to the unannounced appearance of
someone challenging my claim. They could have had
no way of knowing how I would react. And so they had
to include in their plot something which would force
my hand, keep me out of the law courts. Something
that would make me docile. A form of blackmail...

Yes, that was it! Jason had used the word himself.
Had he been trying to prompt me? Had he gently and
carefully been telling me not of his position but my
own?

I opened my eyes. There was the meadow, the long
grass dappled by the wind. There the river, its surface
white tufted. Nothing had changed. And yet everything
had changed!

I turned to look at Jason. He was standing where I
had left him. Handsome. Perfectly outfitted. A look of
puzzled concern in his dark eyes. And it was all false. I
was sure of it now.

I could not let him believe that I was deceived any
longer.

"How clever of both of you," I said in a clear voice.
"You're to be 'forced' to take the estate away from me.
And you can be certain that I won't take legal steps
because were I to do so and be successful, my mother
will do what she 'threatened' to do. Tell the world my
father was a murderer. Destroy the only thing that's
left of him, his reputation! How stupid I was not to see

it at once. I'm the one who has been blackmailed, not you. And I've been blackmailed by two people, not one. You're both in this together, aren't you? What a fool I must have seemed. What an utter fool!"

Strangely enough, Jason made no attempt to defend himself. Even if he had, I would not have stayed to listen. Holding the skirts of my gown high, I ran to the house as though it could offer me some protection. There was a door set deep in the wall facing the terrace and, although its rusty hinges rebelled, I managed to tug it open and found myself in a long, uncarpeted hallway, veiled in dust. The only light came from a window at the end. When I had reached it I found myself looking out at the same courtyard I had seen from my bedroom.

My eyes were nearly blind with unshed tears and it was a few minutes before I saw the narrow stairway. I ran up it like one possessed, although it was clear that Jason did not intend to follow me. There was a door at the top of the stairs and when I pushed it open, I found myself in the corridor outside my bedroom.

Never had I felt so much in need of refuge. Throwing myself onto the bed, I lay without thinking for a long time. Conflicting emotions warred inside me. Outrage. Disappointment. Fear. And all sprang from the same source. I had been deceived by everyone. By my father. Jason. David. How could I trust my instincts ever again? I felt as though my life had been shred to tatters and that I would never be whole again.

Gradually, however, I found that I could think more clearly. There had to be a way out of the situation I found myself in. Or if there were not, at least I could discover the truth. I realized that was the one thing I had to know. This house might be lost to me. My fortune with it. But I would know the truth if it took me the rest of my life. Somehow I would force my mother to produce the person who claimed to have seen my father murder his own brother.

But how? What weapons had I? As Jason had said there was only one way to force her hand. No, not her hand alone now. For he was in this as deeply as she. There was only one way to force *their* hands and that was to contest Jason's claim. Which meant the case had to be brought to court. And I knew that my mother's threat was no idle one. She would enjoy seeing my father's name smeared publicly. There was no way he could defend himself now. That was why they had waited until he was dead.

And then I remembered the letters!

How could I have forgotten them? There was a chance that somewhere in those pages lay the truth!

Throwing myself from the bed, I ran to the portmanteau which set where Rose had left it in the corner by the oak cabinet. My hands shook as I touched the cover. Rose had taken only my clothing from it. I had watched her put each piece away. The letters had to still be inside.

But they were not!

Nothing was there. Nothing!

For a moment my head spun and I tasted blood on my lip where I had bitten it. Then, like someone deranged, I ran to the bell rope which hung beside my bed and pulled it over and over again.

The rope was still in my hand when a knock sounded at the door and Rose entered. The expression on her face was like a mirror and I saw myself as she did, hair disheveled, my cheeks stained with tears.

"Shut the door behind you!" I commanded.

She did as I told her and then came toward me hesitantly.

"Are you all right, Miss?"

"Where is the parcel of letters?" I demanded. It was

all I could do to keep from shaking her.

"Letters, Miss?"

"The letters that were in this!" I cried, flinging myself across the room to raise the cover of the chest. "You can't pretend you didn't see them! I put the parcel there myself just before I left London. It was tucked beneath the shawl."

"Yes, I remember," Rose said in a frightened voice. "It was there. A small package of papers tied with a grey ribbon..."

"Where are they now?" I said. "Tell me where you put them."

"I left them where they were, Miss," she whispered. "If they're not there now, it's none of my doing."

I believed her. There was nothing but honesty in her blue eyes. The fury that had seized me fled as suddenly as it had come and I sank to the floor, covering my eyes with my hands.

"Whatever is wrong, Miss?" Rose cried, falling to her knees beside me.

"Someone has stolen them," I told her. "Someone must have come into this room while I was gone and taken them. And they were all I had, Rose. They were all I had."

Chapter Eight

AN ICY SELF control followed my outburst. At my command Rose summoned Mallick. By the time he appeared I had arranged my hair and gown and donned the black pelisse. If my demand that I be provided with transportation to Oxford at once struck him as odd, he did not show it.

"Mr. David has taken the tilbury, Miss," he told me.

"What else is there?" I said sharply.

"No proper conveyance for a young lady, I'm afraid, Miss. Only the gelding that Mr. David keeps for hunting."

"Is there a side saddle?"

He nodded. "The mistress rides from time to time. But..."

"See that the horse is saddled and ready within ten minutes," I told him in a steady voice.

"If you will allow me to consult the mistress. . . ."

"I am mistress here," I told him sharply. "This house and everything in it belongs to me. Or perhaps you were not aware of that fact."

Bowing, Mallick left the room. Not a flicker of emotion had crossed his face but I felt, somehow, that there was a certain insolence in the way in which he turned away from me.

Whether there was or not, the horse was waiting in exactly ten minutes time when I left the house, passing through the outer courtyard. The boy who was holding the reins was the same lad I had seen wheeling my grandfather in the Bath chair two days before. The sight of him reminded me of the promise I had made to the old man the night before. But there was no time to think of that now. My mind was set on Oxford and the telegram I intended to send to Mr. Harlow, asking him to come to Ludden Hall at once.

The next hour passed quickly. The gelding was a lively animal and I was glad that my father had insisted that I become an accomplished horsewoman. Guiding the beast down the long hill to the town required an expertise seldom demanded during my morning outings along Rotten Row in Hyde Park.

Still, I must have presented a strange figure as I rode down the High, a woman in mourning costume on a high spirited horse. The self control I had imposed on myself was wearing thin and, as I dismounted by the gate to Magdalen and left the reins in the hands of a grimy boy who agreed to watch him for a penny, I realized that unless Professor Rankin was available and willing to help me, I would have to search the town for the place from which a telegram could be sent.

Luckily the professor was in his rooms when I was led there by the porter. A scholar was with him, a young man with spotty features, who left as soon as I appeared at a nod from the white haired don.

"My dear," Professor Rankin said as soon as we were alone. "What has happened? I thought you had returned to London."

As soon as I had taken the chair to which he led me, I told him everything in a voice which often threatened to break.

"My dear child," he said when I had finished. And then, as he had done the night I had dined with him, he offered me a glass of wine.

It steadied me.

"What am I to do?" I asked him.

"I think you would be right to have your solicitor here," he assured me. "If you will excuse me for a moment, I will see that the message is sent. You say Mr. Harlow has offices at Lincoln's Inn."

He was not gone for more than two minutes, but they seemed an eternity. I felt a furious impatience, but to do what I did not know.

"And now, my dear," the professor said, taking a chair opposite me and holding out one hand, "you must calm yourself."

"How can I do that?" I cried. "My father. . . ."

"It is not possible that he could have murdered his brother," the professor said in a low voice. "We must begin with that fact firmly established. Trust me, my dear. Your father was a spirited fellow when he was young and he possessed a temper, as do most of us, but he would not have murdered anyone. Do you believe me?"

"Yes," I murmured. "I believe you."

"Would you like to have me send for David?" the professor asked. "I know where he can be found at this hour. From what you have told me, I think that any information he could give us would be useful."

"I don't want to see him," I murmured.

"Surely you can't believe that he would be part of this—this plot. Granted that he and I have met on the academic plane only, but I was his tutor when he was an undergraduate and I believe I know something of his character."

"He loves his mother," I said bitterly. "No matter what she claims, he will defend her."

"Just as you defend your father? With no doubts? No hesitations?"

The question was too apt. For I did doubt. He had kept so much from me. I shook my head, unable to answer.

"Don't you see," I said. "I can't trust anyone. Ever again. Not even him."

"But you have come to me," Professor Rankin reminded me gently.

"There is no way you could be involved in this," I told him. "You can be dispassionate."

"Your father was my dearest friend," the professor said. "Both of us are tied to him in much the same manner. As a consequence we can follow only one course. We must defend him."

"But we know he was innocent!" I cried. "Not only because we loved him, but because of the letters. Someone took them. There must have been a reason. They must have proved his innocence."

"They might have seemed to make him guilty," the professor reminded me. "If he did, in fact, love Grace Evans and she him, then whatever was written between them might be precisely the sort of evidence that your mother and the man who calls himself your cousin need."

My return to Ludden Hall late that afternoon was far more decorous than my leaving it had been for Professor Rankin insisted that I take a hired phaeton

while he arranged for the gelding to be ridden back by
one of the grooms at the college. The manner in which I
had ridden into Oxford had not escaped notice,
however. Doubtless Mallick had informed David of
my strange behavior for he was waiting outside the
house, his face drawn in angry lines as the coachman
helped me from the carriage. I saw his eyes sweep the
breadth of my skirt which was, no doubt, covered with
dust, but I threw back my head as I went toward him. If
he had been the friend he pretended to be to me, I
would not have been forced to flee to Oxford as I had.

Without speaking, he opened the small oak door
inside the larger one and we went into the front
courtyard. The rosy brick of the walls of the house
shone warm in the dying sunlight and I felt that now
familiar sense of having come home. I paused,
breathing deeply of the roses, disregarding my companion.

"Perhaps," David said, "you would like to explain
your behavior before we go in and join the others."

"And I think that I have done more than my share of
confiding in you," I said tartly.

The hours spent with Professor Rankin had
rekindled my confidence. Together we had looked at
all the possibilities—the worst along with the best—
and the rationality we had shared had restored my
confidence. The professor, like my father, had the
ability to make me believe that as long as I did not lose
my head all would be well. That and his conviction that
my father would never have been capable of murder or,
for that matter, the fraud with which he had been
charged, had given me back my sense of purpose.
Furthermore, before I had left his rooms a telegram
from Mr. Harlow had arrived stating simply that he
would arrive at Ludden Hall as soon as possible.

But I did not intend to tell David this. Neither did I
propose to repeat to him what Jason had told me that

morning. For all I knew he was already aware of the blackmail with which I was being threatened. I remembered bitterly that, although he had told me the night before that he would share whatever information his mother gave him with me, he had been off to his college this morning without seeing me.

David had, at least, the sensitivity to flush when I rebuked him.

"I wasn't fair, I know," he told me. "But my conversation with my mother last night upset me, and when I found you with Grandfather. . . ."

"Why did it upset you?" I interrupted him.

"He's full of stories," David said. "Some of them true and some not. Furthermore, he hates my mother. He's a perverse old man."

"As it happens," I said stiffly, "I was referring to your talk with your mother. But since you've mentioned Bertie. . . ."

"That's just the sort of foolishness he shouldn't be encouraged in!" David snapped. "He's your grandfather, and no matter what strange requests he may make, that's what he should be called."

"Since he *is* my grandfather and not yours, I believe I will call him whatever name pleases him," I retorted.

It was absurd, I knew, that we should stand there discussing what I should call the old man when so much of importance needed to be said. But we were angry with one another and I guessed that whether we knew it or not, we were taking advantage of a petty quarrel to get rid of some of the animosity between us.

David shrugged his broad shoulders and I noticed that he had apparently returned from his college in such a hurry that he had not thought to discard the scholar's gown which hung like a cape over his black suit.

"Did you know," I asked him, determined to press

the issue one step further, "that your mother intends to have him put away?"

"I'd be sorry to see it happen," David muttered, "although, I assure you, such a step would be justified. Certainly he's not senile. But you don't know anything about him, although probably you found him a mine of malicious stories about my mother."

Rather than diminishing our annoyance with one another, this topic of conversation, at least, was stirring us both to a fury, and I knew that soon one or the other of us would say something which would never be forgiven. Disillusioned as I was with David, I did not care to think of him as a life-long enemy.

"I don't need to depend on malicious stories," I told him in a low voice. "And now I think I'll go to my room. I'm rather tired. Perhaps you'll let the housekeeper know that there may be one other guest at dinner. I can't be certain when he'll arrive, but Mr. Harlow will be here sometime tonight."

And then, remembering the night before when I had appeared unannounced, I added: "He'll be staying here so a room should be prepared, as well."

David was staring at me incredulously, and as I started up the gravel path to the house, he took my arm and whirled me about to face him. Such a show of force was so uncharacteristic that I did not protest.

"You've taken a good deal on yourself, haven't you?" he said. "And without as much as knowing the workings of this house. As it happens, there is no housekeeper. Rose and her sister Miriam take care of everything and they certainly aren't prepared to provide a dinner party for five people."

"It won't be a 'dinner party,'" I retorted. "And you can't ask me to believe that those two young girls...."

"There was a cook until a short time ago," David said, and there was something in his voice that told me he wished he had not broached the subject.

"How long ago?" I demanded.

"The day before yesterday," David muttered. "She left because of—of what happened to my mother."

"The laudanum?"

"It was all that Mallick could do to keep the two girls on," David told me. "Besides, what business does Harlow have here?"

"My business," I replied. "Not the least of which concerns a parcel of letters which were stolen from my room this morning. Letters that were the property of my father. It seems obvious that since I am intended to be made a victim in more than one way...."

"Why do you call yourself a victim?" David demanded. "You've disappointed me, Ruth. I didn't anticipate such hysterical behavior from you."

"By now you must realize that I'm in a situation which demands that my lawyer be here," I told him grimly.

"Because some letters were misplaced?"

"Stolen. And there's a good deal more. Don't pretend you don't know about it."

His hands fell from my arms.

"You must believe me," he said slowly. "I came away from my mother last night knowing nothing more than you told me yourself on the train. She told me that she had private information that the real heir to the estate was living in Canada and that she considered it her duty to communicate with him. She seemed to feel that there was no doubt but that his documents—the papers which prove his identity— would be authenticated, and she assured me that she held no ill will toward you."

I laughed bitterly.

"I know," David said gently. "It can't seem that way to you when you're faced with losing everything. And of course I laughed myself when she said that she was simply interested in seeing justice done. She hated your father. That's the reason for all of this. If she had told me what she intended to do before she wrote to this man, I would have tried to keep her from interfering. Even though I didn't know you at the time..."

"You don't share her commendable concern for justice then?" I taunted him. And yet I believed what he was saying. And in the moment of believing I remembered how Jason had deceived me and steeled myself. Why was it so difficult to strip myself of trust? At the most it was a fool's virtue.

"I want to help you, Ruth."

For a moment our eyes met and then, shaking my head, I turned and went toward the house.

Chapter Nine

IT WOULD HAVE been easy to have gone directly to my
room. Easy and comforting for no doubt Nelly would
be waiting for me. There was nothing I would have
liked better than to slip into my dressing gown and
drink a cup of tea with Nelly to comfort me.

But when I came to the door of the sitting room, I
knew I had to go in and encounter my mother and
Jason. I had to show both of them that their threat had
not frightened me, that I was in no mood to capitulate
to their demands. As I paused in the dusky great hall to
brush the dust from my black skirt, David appeared
from behind me and offered his arm. Together we

entered the long, garishly furnished room where the late sunlight streamed through long windows.

Tea had already been served. The tray was set on a low table in front of my mother who was dressed in an elaborate gown of green silk. About her throat hung a necklace of seed pearls, which had been among the jewelry I had brought to her and on her wrist I saw the serpent bracelet. Jason, his face pale above his high collar, rose as we entered and bowed ever so slightly, while my grandfather, a wizened figure in the wing chair by the fire, smiled broadly and pointed with one clawlike hand at the settee beside him.

"Sit here beside old Bertie, gel!" he exclaimed in a creaking voice. "I was telling them you'd come back in good time for tea. Young gels like their tea."

I sank down obediently beside him, but not before I had caught the glance which David and his mother exchanged. Impossible to interpret what bit of information it was meant to convey. As for Jason, he remained standing, his face set in grim lines.

It was an awkward situation and no one except my grandfather made any pretense that it was otherwise. As for the old man, the light-heartedness of his mood could have been explained, I thought, by the knowledge that in me he had found an ally. He was rambling on in what might, in any other circumstance, have been an amusing way concerning a houseparty he had once attended at the Duke of Bedford's country house when my mother, having poured both David and me our tea, interrupted him firmly.

"And now, Father," she said, "I think that you ought to rest until dinner."

The metamorphosis in the old man was pitiful. His face wrinkled like a child's and he glanced around himself frantically in a way which emphasized his helplessness.

"I'd like to have him stay," I said quietly.

"No doubt you would," my mother retorted and then added, catching David's eye: "Oh, very well, but it's your responsibility if he exhausts himself."

"You'll tell us when you feel tired, won't you?" I murmured, taking the old man's hand in my own.

He nodded thankfully, but kept silent, obviously warned that his garrulity was not welcome.

"I expect you'd like to tell us all about your unexpected trip to Oxford," my mother said in a flat voice. "I scarcely expected that you had come here from London for the express purpose of making a public display of yourself. Or perhaps your father would have seen nothing unusual in a young woman in mourning riding horseback into town without even bothering to change into a riding habit."

Jason had moved to a position by the mantlepiece which enabled him to avoid my eye and look directly at her. I wondered if it struck him as it did me how beautiful she was. The years had done little to her features except fine them to the bone and her cheeks were tinged with pink, although whether by nature or artifice I could not tell. Her auburn hair was as thick as my own and was arranged in such a way that a few ringlets had escaped from the coil at the nape of her neck. I remembered ruefully how, in my first flush of anger after I had received her terse note in London, I had thought to put her to shame with my own youth. How disheveled I must look beside her now. And she was right to suggest that I had behaved like a hoyden with my sudden flight that morning. If, with those few words, she had hoped to make me feel gauche, she had succeeded.

But I would let nothing repress my defiance of her, I promised myself.

"If you and Mr. Bramwell have had occasion to talk

privately today," I replied, "I expect you are well aware that I might have good reason to go about my own business."

"Up to something they are, the two of them," my grandfather muttered.

I silenced him with a glance.

"Perhaps you would like to tell us about your 'business,'" my mother said, leaning back in her chair, staring at me through heavy-lidded eyes. "That is if it concerns us."

I wished that I could see Jason's face. Surely he must have informed her by now that I was well aware of the terms they had imposed on me.

"I went to Oxford to speak to an old friend of my father's," I said and then waited to see what their reaction would be. Because I wanted, more than anything else, to make them believe that I had resources of my own.

My mother raised her thin eyebrows but did not speak. It was David who said, "Professor Rankin?" in a tone of surprise.

I nodded. "He is a gentleman for whose opinion I have considerable respect," I said. "And then, of course, he knew my father from a very early age."

Jason shifted his position. Still I could not see his face, but I sensed a certain discomfort. Was he wondering, perhaps, if the professor could provide some sort of refutation to the claim that my father had been a murderer? I had quite deliberately made reference to "an early age." Let them wonder whether or not Professor Rankin had been an intimate of my father's since childhood.

Whether David knew better I could not tell. He seemed strangely ill at ease, pacing catlike about the cluttered room while his tea cooled in its cup.

"So you went to this man for advice," my mother

said thoughtfully.

I suppose it was then that I realized that, as far as she was concerned, we were not to discuss the terms under which I was presumably to capitulate. The initiative would have to be mine. But should I take it?

"I went to him for information," I hedged, determined, if nothing else, to make her as uncomfortable as she was making me. And all the time my mind was worrying the matter of what should or should not be said. She and Jason and I, at least, knew how matters stood. But David had claimed to know nothing more than I had told him the night before in the train. Would it be to my advantage to put the terms of my blackmail before him squarely and let them refute it if they could? Whatever I did it must be to my advantage.

"And was he—helpful?" my mother asked quietly. We might have been discussing the weather.

I was too absorbed in my own thoughts to answer her at once and I was only faintly aware that David had said something to her sotto voce and that he sounded angry.

The question I had to decide was whether to speak openly then or wait until I was alone with her. Or perhaps it would be wisest to wait until I had had the opportunity to talk to Mr. Harlow, to get his advice and then decide whether or not to take it.

If I did speak at that moment, what would I say? Should I demand to know who it was who claimed to be a witness to the so-called murder of my uncle? If I could believe Jason, she had refused to tell him. I did not, of course, believe that there was any such person, or if there were it was someone willing to perjure himself for some share in the fortune she was determined to strip from me.

No, if I were to demand to know who her informant was she would probably laugh. Or suggest that if I wanted to know I should bring the case of my claim to Ludden Hall and all the rest to court so that everything could become public. Perhaps, I thought, the matter of money was secondary to her. Perhaps she hoped that I would defy her and give her no recourse but to destroy my father's reputation. For that was what would happen, of course. Even if Jason's claim was proved to be false, even if her "witness" could be proved to be lying—although how that would be possible after forty years I did not know—the scandal would not be forgotten. The utter injustice of what she was doing made me want to kill her.

And of course that was another thing. If all of this were to come to law she could claim that I had attempted just that. In order to keep her quiet, she would say, I laced her tea with laudanum. A doctor could give witness to the fact that she had been poisoned, that someone had apparently attempted to kill her. It would be of little importance that I was certain she had taken the drug herself. Nothing could be proved. In all of this nothing could be proved beyond a doubt except the validity of Jason's claim. And from what I knew of him now, I was certain that he would insist on taking the case to court if I resisted.

I clenched my fingers and only then realized that my grandfather's hand was still in mine. He returned the pressure and I thought I saw understanding in his pale blue eyes. It occurred to me that since I did not believe that he was senile, I had to talk to him alone. Tell him everything that had happened. He had made it clear enough that there was no love between himself and my mother. He feared her, perhaps even hated her. And it could be that he might be able to give me useful information. Perhaps the fear of this was what had driven her to threaten him with an asylum. I determined to find the location of his room from Rose and go to him at night when we could be undisturbed.

I realized that the others were staring at me, silent, and remembered the question that my mother had put to me.

"Professor Rankin was very helpful," I said. "Among other things he saw to it that a telegram was sent to Mr. Harlow who will arrive here this evening."

If I had thought that my mother would be disconcerted by this news, I was mistaken. Her lips curled in a strange, vague smile as though she was secretly delighted. The niggling thought came to me that she might know my solicitor better than I had thought. Granted that he had claimed to have met her only years ago when she had still lived with my father. But I remembered now how nervous he had been when I had asked him about her. At the time I had put his discomposure down to delicacy, but now I began to wonder. What, after all, had been the message she had sent by David to him?

I was aware of a sliding feeling of exhaustion. Releasing my grandfather's hand, I rose from the settee.

"I believe that I will go upstairs now," I said. "I hope that Nelly has been made comfortable. I would like to speak with her."

"Nelly?"

My mother seemed genuinely puzzled.

I felt as though a cold wind had begun to blow through the room.

"She was supposed to arrive this afternoon with the rest of my luggage," I said in a voice which I did not recognize as my own.

For the first time Jason spoke.

"I can assure you," he said, frowning, "that no one has arrived here since you left. Whoever this Nelly is, she is not at Ludden Hall."

*   *   *

"You say that Nelly was reluctant to come here with you earlier this week," Mr. Harlow said in a reasonable voice. "Isn't it quite possible that she simply could not bring herself to join you now? In a word, isn't it quite the most probable thing that she sent your luggage on by rail and remained at Sloan Square? Doubtlessly you will have a letter from her tomorrow."

"That's quite impossible," I said more shortly than I meant to sound. Nelly knew when I left her yesterday that she was to join me. She made it quite clear that she would prefer not to stay in this house, but she knew that I needed her. Nelly would never have failed me this way. Never!"

I hoped that Mr. Harlow would not take my rejection of his explanation personally. It had been kind of him to come on the basis of a telegram which had offered no explanation for what some solicitors might have considered an unreasonable request.

He had arrived in a hired carriage only minutes before and I had led him directly to the morning room where we sat in the oak paneled shadows of late afternoon. In an hour we would have to join the others at dinner, but until then I wanted to keep him to myself. His familiar florid face encased in mutton chop whiskers and his benevolent eyes magnified by his thick spectacles were as reassuring to me as any sight could be at that particular time.

"Something must have happened to her," I said in a low voice. "I think that we should notify the police."

Mr. Harlow's thick fingers moved restlessly up and down the length of his gold watch chain.

"You are in a highly excited state, my dear," he said soothingly. "If you will take my advice, you will wait until tomorrow. Then, of course, if a letter or a telegram has not arrived it will be time to get in contact with your own household. But, if I may be frank, I do not believe that will be necessary. Your nurse may have reached a decision not to come after you left her. Second thoughts, don't you know."

His words reminded me of my mother's response when I had indicated alarm on hearing that Nelly had not arrived.

"She's afraid to come, of course," she had said with a hint of triumph in her voice.

"Nonsense," David had said. "Why on earth should she be afraid?"

"Because she knows that I suspect her of having tried to poison me," my mother had retorted.

My grandfather had shaken his white head slowly. "Not enough spunk," he muttered regretfully. "Saw the woman myself. Not enough spunk by half."

My mother flashed him an angry look.

"She had the opportunity," she said sharply, turning to look at me. "You must remember that she returned to this room just as you were leaving. To fetch her purse, she said."

"Why on earth would Ruth's nurse want to poison you?" David demanded. "This is no time to make hysterical accusations."

"She always loathed me," my mother said in a low voice as though she had suddenly lapsed into a private conversation with herself. "She wasn't *my* choice as a nurse. Oh, no. He hired her. There was a private arrangement between them. She went to him with every bit of tattle she managed to pick up. She was nothing better than a spy. No, she was worse than that. He allowed her to take care of the child as she saw fit. If there was any question, she went to him."

The spite in her voice repelled me. I knew that she was speaking of my father and that the child she referred to so obliquely was me. And it was disconcerting to be spoken of as though I were another person and not that child grown. Although perhaps that was how it seemed to her. Grudgingly I was forced to admit to myself that if what she said was true, if my father had taken all motherly functions out of her hands, she might have had good reason to resent Nelly. But, I reminded myself, if my father had done that it must have been because he did not think her fit in some way to care for me, to make decisions about my welfare.

"Can't blame the man," my grandfather said rearing himself up in his chair like an animated scarecrow. "Never cared for children, did you, Miss? Young David here was brought up by nurses. That's the truth and don't deny it. If he don't remember, I do. And then sent off to school as soon as he was old enough to be taken in."

David turned on his heel and went to stand by one of the long windows as though intent on something going on outside. His shoulders were stiff, and I wondered just how much challenge his loyalty to his mother could endure.

As for her, she shrugged her shoulders. I did not know her well, but I imagined that was how she greeted facts which could not be refuted. How such a response must have infuriated my father, fond as he had been of argument based on careful logic. I had glanced at Jason, standing silent by the fire. He was watching her, his eyes narrowed. Was he admiring her, I wondered, or regretting that he had thrown his lot in with someone so obviously interested in no one but herself?

Mr. Harlow's cough returned me to the present.

"Will you wait until tomorrow, my dear?" he said. "Try to put Nelly out of your mind for the present?"

"I don't know if I can," I told him frankly. "First the letters and then her...."

"I'm afraid," he said stiffly, "that I do not understand your reference. I think it would be best if you explained what has happened since I last saw you to put you in such·a state."

He was right, of course. If I wanted him to advise me, I had to tell him everything.

When I began it was with the sense that it would all be very difficult to explain, but in the end there seemed to be surprisingly little to say. I was very careful to be clear. What had happened was put to him in chronological order, just as it had occurred. Mr. Harlow listened intently, the fingers of one hand moving restlessly across the knee of his trousers as though he wished to take notes. When I had finished he sat for a few minutes, staring past me and I guessed that he was filing the facts in his mind as though they were so many index cards.

"An astonishing story," he said finally. "If, of course, it is true."

"Of course it's true," I said. "Jason told me...."

"Ah, but that is just the point, isn't it?" he interrupted. "Everything you told me—everything of importance, that is—was told to you by a man we know absolutely nothing about."

He was right, of course. How odd that until now I had not realized it. It had been Jason who had told me the details of why he was in London. And again, today, it had been Jason who had told me that he was being blackmailed by my mother to press his claim. It had been Jason who had made me see that if I wished to protect my father's name I could make no formal protest.

"You have been here at Ludden Hall for nearly twenty-four hours," Mr. Harlow continued, pressing the fingers of each hand against one another. "And yet at no time have you and your mother spoken directly to the matter. Does that not strike you as strange?"

"Jason is her—her agent," I protested. "She told him what to say."

"How can we be sure of that?"

Mr. Harlow spoke crisply, as though he were addressing the bar. There was little about him of the genial gentleman I had known in the past.

"She claims to have been poisoned," I reminded him. "That threat, at least, comes directly from her."

"I thought you said that David told you about her suspicions."

I hesitated. "Yes, that's true. And all the more proof that she prefers to use her weapons indirectly. Besides, why should both Jason and David be lying?"

"I did not suggest they were, my dear." His voice took on some of its customary gentleness. It was as though a mask had slipped aside for a moment and was now being carefully replaced. But, of course, that was nonsense. I was being fanciful. This was the man my father had trusted with his affairs and, of course, I could trust him, too.

"I simply propose," he went on slowly, "that before we take any further steps we hear all this from your mother directly."

"She would deny it, of course," I told him. "After all, she's involved in something criminal."

Mr. Harlow shook his head slowly. "That would be very difficult to prove, I'm afraid, even if what this— this stranger says is true. If she feels that she has proof that your father was involved in—er, murder, she has the right to suggest that, under certain circumstances, the facts must come out. Were he alive, of course, she would be under a legal obligation to divulge what she knows. Now that he is dead, however, there is no such obligation. But she is still perfectly free to warn you, as she has apparently done, that. . . ."

"You sound as though you believe that my father did kill his brother!" I cried.

It was nearly dusk now. I could scarcely see Mr. Harlow's face. And yet I could not be bothered with light.

"Do you believe it?" I pressed him.

He cleared his throat. "I find it most unlikely," he answered. "Aside from what I knew of his character, I can see no reason for this—this witness to have remained silent for so many years if he is willing now to step forward. If he had wished justice to be done, he would have spoken out forty years ago. Even if he had no concern for justice and wished only to harm your father he would scarcely have waited until the man he hated was—er, beyond reach, in a manner of speaking."

It must have been that I had expected his first reaction to be one of total disbelief, for I felt as though he had betrayed me.

"It's all a lie!" I cried, springing from my chair. "How can you treat it seriously?"

"In the legal world lies must be taken as seriously as truths," Mr. Harlow said ponderously. "Even more seriously, perhaps. In this case, particularly so since your mother's—er, witness, if there is such a person, can make his charge with impunity."

I felt as though I were being sucked into a whirlpool of rage and despair.

"I don't understand you," I said in a whisper.

"It might be difficult to bring a charge of libel," Mr. Harlow explained, "since the man who is being accused of murder is already dead."

I clenched my hands until my nails bit into my skin.

"You sound as though you were saying that we must give her and Jason what they want," I said incredulously.

"Not at all, my dear," he assured me. "Not at all. I am simply explaining to you that they have managed to put themselves in a very strong position. If I am to defend your interests properly, I must know a good deal more about the matter than I do now. Hearsay from a stranger is not enough."

"What do you propose then?" I demanded.

"My clerk is in the process of attempting to determine whether Mr. Bramwell is, in fact, the heir," Mr. Harlow told me. "I thought the matter to be of sufficient importance to hire a private inquiry agent to assist him. That side of things can, I think, be safely left in their hands. But there is a good deal that you and I can do, my dear. Indeed, I'm very glad that you called me here. It is not as though the estate involved is of little consequence. We must, among other things, make every effort to recover your father's letters. And we must insist on an interview with your mother as soon as possible."

My mother did not appear for dinner, sending word by Mallick that she was feeling a bit unwell. Mr. Harlow and I looked at one another helplessly, for it had been agreed between us that we would talk to her after dinner. It occurred to me that in all probability she had guessed that we would want to see her alone and that she had used this device to avoid an awkward interview. However, I reassured myself, she could not avoid us indefinitely.

On hearing that his mother was to remain in her room, David had hurried upstairs with a proper show of filial concern, only to return in a few minutes wearing a curiously grim expression. It was left to Jason to ask if there was any need for concern to which David replied tersely that she was "resting."

My grandfather joined us in the dining room, debonair in musty evening dress and carrying himself in a more spritely manner than I had seen him display before. Although the rest of us obviously felt uncomfortable together, the old man set out to make himself the life and soul of the party, sitting at the head of the table with me at his right since, as he put it, a pretty "gel" at a meal was as good as a fine wine when it came to "perking up the palate."

Rose served the meal which consisted of a thin soup, sole with a passable sauce, a nicely roasted sirloin, trifle and even a savory. It was a commendable effort and I told her so as she cleared away the plates. I was glad enough for the dinner to come to an end since I had had little appetite and my grandfather's high spirits, having been spurred by the wine which he had helped himself to generously, were beginning to wear on me. The stories that he told of a past in which all the women were beautiful and witty and all the men handsome and fond of pleasure would have intrigued me at any other time. It was certainly true that he appeared to be holding the interest of the three other men and Mr. Harlow was seen once to smile. And I could not help but be pleased that my presence had apparently given him the courage to join us since, as he explained wryly, he usually took "pap" in his bedroom for his evening meal. But I was in no mood for anything except introspection and as soon as I could, I excused myself and left the gentlemen to their port.

I would have preferred to go to the morning room, but there was neither light nor fire there and so I was forced to take my coffee in the cluttered sitting room, a room so redolent of my mother's presence that I could not be comfortable in it.

When Rose came with the tray, her face flushed scarlet with the effort she had made, I spoke again of how excellent the meal had been, and inquired if any effort was being made to replace the cook who had so recently deserted the house.

"No, Miss. Not as I know of," she began, and then went on in a rush to explain that she and her sister were giving their notice as well.

"It's not just the extra work, Miss," she explained. "There's something not right here what with you losing your letters the way you did and the mistress talking about poisoning though I know as should that she dosed herself and has done a good many nights since I came here. It's the responsibility, Miss. It's like I said to my sister after the doctor was here the other night, as long as the mistress won't admit to her habit there's none of us can help her."

"Put down your tray and sit down, Rose," I said in a low voice, my heart pounding as fast as though I had been running. "Are you telling me that Mrs. Bramwell takes laudanum regularly and in considerable doses?"

Rose nodded vigorously. "She'd see me gone if she was to know I'd told you, Miss, but since Della and I are giving notice anyway, there's no reason you shouldn't know. Night after night I've seen her sleeping like the dead with the candles all burning as though there was an entertainment going on."

"Does anyone but yourself know this?" I demanded, leaning forward eagerly.

"Della knows. I tell her everything, I do. And Mr. Mallick, he knows everything, nasty sneaking creature that he is."

"What about David and his lordship?"

Rose shook her head. "Innocent as babes they are," she commented.

"Why didn't you tell the doctor this?" I asked her.

"Well, there was my job to think of, wasn't there?" Rose said almost pertly. And then, smoothing her apron: "I'm sorry, Miss, but it's that upset I've been."

"If she were to bring a charge against someone," I said earnestly, "if she were to go to court to claim she had been poisoned, would you tell the truth?"

"Oh, Miss! I wouldn't like to promise anything like that. My Mam wouldn't be half angry."

"It won't come to that, I'm sure," I said reassuringly. "Now, Rose, you must do this for me. Stay on for a while. I'll see that someone is brought in to help you and your sister. I need you."

But I could extract no promise from her and she left the sitting room shaking her head just as Jason was coming in.

Rising, I started toward the door for apparently he had left the others at the table and I had no intention of a tête-à-tête with him. Besides, I wanted to be alone to consider the implications of my mother's addiction. Somewhere at the back of my mind lurked the conviction that everything that had happened would have to be reconsidered.

"Please stay for just a minute, Ruth."

Jason's voice was low pitched, but it was clear that he was making a command rather than a request. It was not by chance, I thought, that he remained standing before the closed door in such a way that it would have been necessary to push him aside if I intended to leave.

"I want you to know that the assumption you made this morning was totally false," he said.

I avoided meeting those dark eyes. They had misled me before. Just so I attempted to disregard the note of sincerity in his voice. After all, he was only saying what I had expected him to say. This morning I had fled from him because I anticipated that it would pain me to hear him lie. And I had been right. There was pain.

"I realize that you probably don't believe me," he

went on as I stared with determination at the bold, floral pattern of the carpet. "I spent a good part of the afternoon with your mother, trying to force her to tell me where she got her information about me. And in the process of our little—talk, I came to the conclusion that she believes everything she says. Someone has managed to convince her not only that the estate is mine, but that your father. . . ."

"Don't say the word," I warned him, raising my eyes. "There will be no further discussion about it between us."

He looked at me steadily.

"Then there is nothing left to say but this. I intend to return to Canada as soon as possible. But only with your permission, Ruth."

"My permission!"

He had disconcerted me completely.

"You may have to suffer the consequences if I go," he said, "and that is not a threat. It is a warning. Your mother may well be a charming woman in some circumstances, but two hours spent with her today convinced me that she is seriously unbalanced. I told her that I found her interest in 'justice' suspect and her response was hysterical. Nevertheless I went on to explain to her that I have no need of a fortune which will bring so much misery to you."

I did not want to believe him and yet, as always, he was convincing. Disturbingly so. Why, if he were in league with her, if all this were lies, did he bother? Between them, they had me well and truly in a trap. What need was there for him to try to prove any altruism on his part? Why did he need my sympathy?

"Do you expect me to believe that you would really turn your back on several hundred thousand pounds and this house as well?" I demanded.

"Willingly, I assure you," he said quietly. "I am far from destitute."

"And yet you traveled three thousand miles."

He shrugged. "It is my misfortune that I did so," he replied. "Although I can see that you are determined not to believe that if I stay here now it will only be to protect you. Your mother claims that if I leave she will make the story of what she claims happened forty years ago public. It is my belief that she will do so."

"So nothing has really changed," I said dryly, turning away from him. "You claim not to threaten me, and yet...."

"*She* threatens."

"The consequences are the same," I reminded him.

Going to one of the long windows I looked out into a moonlit night. The wind had risen, bending the poplar trees, while in the sky clouds darted across the faces of the stars.

"Shall I leave England?"

He had come to stand behind me. Too close. His physical presence was strangely disturbing. I shuddered. God help me if I were to fall in love with him, this man who might be my brother. Was that what he was trying to do to me? Did he hope in this way to make me even less likely to press my claim in a courtroom?

"Do you think my mother is mad?" I said out of a sense of desperation, a need to say anything to keep distance between us.

"I said that I believed her to be emotionally unbalanced. She recognizes this herself, or claims to. She spoke to me at length of the torment she has endured during the past sixteen years. This house, she claims, has been her prison."

"There was no need for her to stay here," I protested. "My father told me himself that he had made a financial settlement on her at the time of their separation."

"She says that the amount was so little as to leave her destitute were she to go elsewhere, although what her concept of destitution is I have no idea."

He was standing so close behind me that I seemed to feel the warmth of his breath on my shoulders. And yet I could not move away for were I to do so I had to turn. And, turning, would find myself in his arms.

"Mr. Harlow will be able to prove that information," I said as briskly as I could.

"Ah, the admirable Mr. Harlow. And what is his response to the situation? Has he advised you?"

"I will take my own advice," I snapped. "If your papers are proved valid—with no question, then the estate is yours. Whether you return to Canada or not, it is yours. I would not wish to live on money which was not my own or in a house which is the property of a stranger."

"So I am to be a stranger."

I told myself that if he were to touch me now I would cry out.

"And if your papers cannot be irrefutably proved," I went on quickly, "I will test the matter in court. She can call my father murderer if she will! I will take pleasure in proving her what she is. Thief! Liar!"

Involuntarily I turned as I said the words and saw, over Jason's shoulder, Mallick standing in the doorway, his face in the shadows.

"What are you doing here?" I demanded.

Startled, Jason turned to face the intruder.

"I came to ask if there was anything I could get you, Miss."

Mallick's voice was, as usual, expressionless. How long had he been standing there, I wondered? How much had he heard?

It was Jason who put my thoughts into words. Mallick bowed.

"I'm sorry if I intruded, sir," he said with veiled insouciance.

"Look here," Jason began angrily and started forward. At the same moment Mallick opened the door. Beyond him in the hall a candlelit procession was filing past. My grandfather was being assisted on either side by David and Mr. Harlow.

"Ah, Mallick!" the old man croaked, waving his cane. "Spying as usual, I see!"

His voice was exultant, the words slurred. Obviously he had drunk well and deeply of the port. Holding his ground despite efforts on the part of the two men to move him along, my grandfather addressed me with all the force his voice could carry.

"The man's a rogue, gel!" he declared. "If there's dirty business afoot, you can be sure he's at the bottom of it!"

I had thought to find some sort of quietude in my bedroom, but my mind was as restless as the wind outside and my anxiety concerning Nelly as deep as the shadows which fell on the courtyard below when clouds flew across the moon.

Standing by the window, I tried to sort things in my mind, to tidy it as I would a sewing basket. Nelly was safe at Sloan Square, I told myself, doubtlessly feeling remorseful about not doing as she had been asked. Perhaps she was already planning to take the morning train. At all events there would be a letter from her tomorrow, explaining her absence.

Pretending that one matter, at least, was settled, I drew my dressing gown more tightly about me and went to the window. The wind was heavy now, rattling the panes of glass. How many stormy nights had this house seen, I wondered? I touched the velvet softness of the oak paneling and pressed my face close to it, smelling the perfume of old wood. Why did it have to be that I should love this house so much? The money was important, of course, all those safe investments my father had made over the years. But it was only the loss of this house that made me want to weep. What would Jason do with it? His home was in Canada. He would not come to live here because of a house. Securities could be transferred to other banks. Houses could be sold. How I hated the thought of strangers living here!

I reminded myself that I had determined to make this time one for the solving of problems, or at least the sorting of them. Later there would doubtlessly be time enough for remorse. How strange that I should insist on predicating my thoughts of the future on the validity of Jason's claim. Perhaps if Mr. Harlow had not made it seem so clearly a possibility.

With an effort I forced myself to think of the immediate problems. The revelation that my mother might well be addicted to opium in the form of laudanum needed consideration. Was it possible that the overdose she had taken had been accidental, prompted perhaps by her need to steel herself after our first meeting? No matter what sort of woman she was, it must have been a shock for her to have seen me a grown woman when, in her mind, I must have remained the child she had been forced to leave behind her sixteen years before. My grandfather had accused her of disliking children, but surely she had had some feeling for me. I had only her word for it, of course, that she had had no choice, that my father had insisted that I stay with him. Still, it was logical. She had been guilty of infidelity, which fact alone must have made her seem unfit in his eyes for her to raise me. Nearly as important to him must have been her lack of any intellectual interest and the appalling lack of taste personified by the jewelry her lover had given her. Cruel as it might have been to separate a child from her mother, I could see that to my father it would have seemed necessary.

Very well, then. Seeing me again had been upsetting. If what Rose had told me was true, would it not have been natural that she would have resorted to laudanum? That she would take more than her customary dose? And later, knowing that she could not keep it secret since Rose had found her unconscious, might she not have taken refuge in the only lie which had come to her fogged mind? It might have been only to protect herself that she had claimed that someone else had drugged her.

But did that change matters? The wind had brought rain with it now and was dashing it against the window. The moon had disappeared. Shivering, I drew the heavy drapes, dislodging dust.

I began to pace the room. Such an explanation made her seem less unscrupulous but it did nothing to excuse the role she had played in depriving me of my inheritance. Unless, of course, she had been forced to write the letter, to make the threat to tarnish my father's reputation. That was a possibility I had to consider.

But that would mean that someone had power of some sort over her. Did someone, perhaps, know of her addiction and threaten to make it public? No one could control her supply of the drug since laudanum could be bought without prescription at any chemist. Besides, who else but she would want to hurt me and through me, my father?

The single candle by my bed gutted and nearly died. I went to light another, scarcely aware of what I was doing. My mind was racing.

Perhaps the matter of hurting me was completely beside the point, something thought up by someone who wanted to disguise their own role in this matter. That someone would have to have something to gain. And Jason was that person.

How I hated the memory of how his physical presence had disturbed me. All of this, quite likely, had been his idea. The reluctant heir. I tried to laugh scornfully, but the sound was more like a mourn. I knew nothing about the man except what he had told me, and every word of that was doubtless a lie. His accent indicated that he had at some time in his life lived in Canada, but it was not necessarily true that he had just arrived in this country. Quite possibly he had been living here all along. He could easily have heard of my father's illness and made his plans accordingly. Months ago he could have been scheming with my mother. It needed only my father's death to set the plan into action. Whether he had forced my mother to take part or not, it might be that he was the instigator of the plot. A subtle plot. More devious, perhaps, than she was capable of devising. I realized that I knew little of her except that she could be cold. Sardonic. But was she likely to have found someone who was willing to perjure themselves, to say that they had seen murder done forty years ago for the express purpose of keeping me from making a serious attempt to keep what was mine?

I sat down on the bed and pulled a blanket about me. Someone had seen to lighting a fire earlier, but it was nearly dead now and the wind and rain made the shadowy room seem icy.

And who was this perjurer? That was the most important question of all. My head had begun to ache, but I knew there was no purpose in trying to sleep. The wind seemed to be driving my thoughts before it as it had driven the clouds. If only this mysterious person could be identified, Mr. Harlow or I could talk to him. Apply pressures. Force him to withdraw his offer to testify to a murder which could not have taken place.

Suddenly I thought of the letters. I had assumed that someone had taken them because they might contain some proof of my father's innocence. But could it not be that somewhere in one of them a name had been mentioned, the name of someone Grace Evans had known, the name of the unknown person who was willing to accuse my father of murder?

Yes, I told myself excitedly, that could be it. Whoever it was who claimed to have been witness to the crime must have been someone who had lived nearby, perhaps someone in this very house. And that person had to be over forty. That was the one fact I could be sure of. This man... this woman...

Mallick!

Of course. It had to be he. My grandfather had called him a rogue. Even if he had not I had sensed something ominous about the man from the beginning. Yes, and my grandfather had said more. Drunk he might have been, but when he had told me that Mallick was at the bottom of it, he might well have spoken from some sure knowledge. How frustrating it was not to be able to question him. Now. But given the state in which I had last seen him he was certain to be sleeping deeply. It would do no good to go to him, even if I knew the location of his room.

The thought jarred another into being. I knew the location of one room certainly enough and that was just a step down the corridor. Was it not possible that my mother had dosed herself with laudanum tonight and that she was in a sleep so deep that nothing could awaken her? I could go to her room. Look for the letters. They *might* be there. Any action taken now would relieve me of this agonizing sense of impotency.

Throwing off the blanket, I slipped to the floor and, taking the candle, hurried to the door. If I was wrong, if she were awake or sleeping lightly, I could pretend to want to talk to her. She had not seemed annoyed last night when I had blundered into her room. The interview had given her a chance to try to hurt me and that had obviously given her satisfaction.

The corridor was like a dark tunnel. Even the sound of the wind and rain were muted. But there were sounds. The sounds of an old house. A house from which I had nothing to fear.

There was the door. I turned the brass knob slowly. Once again I saw the overfurnished, befringed room, aglow with candlelight which, reflected in the amber ceiling, gave an impression almost of an inferno in which everything was ablaze. How dangerous it was to keep so many candles lighted when she was asleep, I thought. Did the night hold so many terrors for her?

With an effort I turned my eyes to the bed and saw that it was empty. There was no one in the room.

Where could she be at this time of night? Her absence was strangely like another betrayal. I could not search for the letters when she might, at any moment, return.

Returning to the corridor, I closed the door behind and felt the soft darkness descend. After so much light, the glow of my candle seemed a mockery. And the creaking I had heard before seemed now to be the sound of footsteps. I glanced behind me and seemed to see a shadow moving.

Terror clutched me and I began to run, not in the direction of my room for that was where the shadow was, but toward the front stairs. I opened my mouth to scream and at the same moment felt something strike my head. There was an explosion of agonizing pain and then nothing.

Chapter Ten

I WAS IN bed and someone was smoothing my hair back
from my face. My head ached dully and it seemed
impossible to make the effort required to open my eyes.
The fingers moved softly across my forehead again.

"Nelly," I murmured.

"It's Rose, Miss."

The voice came from very close beside my ear. I
turned my head toward it and forced my eyes open.
Relief was written on Rose's smooth, round face. "Oh,
Miss," she whispered. "I'm so glad you're going to be
all right."

Behind her I could see the pale white light of dawn
pressed against the windows. I closed my eyes against it

and tried to think. Surely my last memory had been of darkness and a shadow.

And then I remembered that agonizing pain.

"What happened?" I murmured. "Did I fall?"

I saw her start to speak and then hesitate. "Perhaps I'd better get the doctor, Miss. He's downstairs with...."

She broke off as though she had been about to say something she should not.

I reached out for her hand and my head throbbed with the effort. Only then did I realize that something was binding my head. There was no need to touch it to know that it was a bandage.

"No," I said. "Don't go. I must know what happened."

"Don't excite yourself, Miss. Please don't. It would be the worst thing in the world for you."

"Am I badly hurt then?" I asked and shifted my body experimentally. Although the movement caused my head to ache even more, it was clear that the rest of me was uninjured.

"No, Miss," Rose said quickly. "You were very lucky, the doctor said. The cane just missed striking you full on the back of the head."

"The cane? What cane?"

She bit her full lip. "Oh, Miss..." she began.

"Can't you see that not knowing what happened is disturbing me far more than anything you could tell me?" I said, speaking as clearly and naturally as possible. "Come, Rose. Are you saying that someone struck me with a cane?"

"Yes, Miss," she whispered. "Mr. David found it on the floor just beside where you were lying unconscious."

Strangely enough I was not surprised. It was as though some vestigial memory of the attack had stayed in my mind.

"But who would do such a thing?" I murmured. "When did David find me? Did he see who attacked me? Tell me everything you know, Rose, or I will get out of this bed and find someone who will."

The threat was enough to convince her that no purpose was being served by hesitation, for she leaned forward in the chair in which she was sitting and pressed my hand tightly.

"Mr. David found you just outside your door when he came upstairs from having seen his lordship to bed. There was no one about. I heard him tell the others that at first he thought you were dead. Oh, Miss, it's all so terribly."

Tears began to stream down her full cheeks.

"No need to cry, Rose," I said a bit impatiently. "I'm quite all right."

For some reason the comment caused her to break into a torrent of tears. Dropping my hand, she raised her apron to her face.

"I'm that frightened, Miss," I heard her say in a muffled voice. "We won't be safe in our beds, not a one of us with a murderer about."

"I'm not dead," I said tartly, "and so it follows there is no murderer."

A fresh flood of tears followed.

"Perhaps," I said, "it might be best if I talked to Mr. Harlow. He will be able to explain this more clearly. Do you know where he is?"

"Oh yes, Miss." The apron descended, exposing a wet frightened face. "He's in the sitting room with the others talking to the Chief Constable."

Why it came as such a shock to me that the police had been called, I do not know. After all, I had, apparently, been attacked.

"They sent for him as soon as they found the body, Miss," Rose wailed. "Oh, it was such a dreadful sight, him lying there at the bottom of the back stairs all sprawled out as though there wasn't a whole bone in him."

Forgetting the pain in my head, I pushed myself into a sitting position.

"Body!" I exclaimed. "Whose body?"

"It was Mallick, Miss. They think it was him as struck you and that he tripped and fell in trying to get away. But my sister says it could be he was pushed because of something that he'd seen. And if that's so, there's not a one of us who's safe!"

It was a strangely subdued Mr. Harlow who informed me that I could avoid an interview with the Chief Constable if I liked on the basis of ill health.

"Indeed, my dear, I urge you to take advantage of your condition," he told me, standing before my bedroom fire, his hands clasped under the tails of his frock coat. I had never seen him so obviously nervous before and indeed he made me quite dizzy rocking, as he was doing, back and forth from toe to heel and back again.

"Why shouldn't I talk to him," I argued, "since I will have to do so sometime?"

I was feeling a good deal more like myself now that I had breakfasted from the well-laden tray Rose had brought to me. The doctor had visited me again and declared that I was a very fortunate young woman. Tall and spare, he fingered my head as though it were a piece of delicate china and pronounced himself satisfied as to my rapid recovery.

"Is there any reason why I shouldn't talk to him?" I repeated now.

"Er—of course not, my dear," Mr. Harlow said. "If you feel quite up to it, that is. Of course you must tell the man—who seems rather a clod, let me say— precisely what happened. The awkwardness comes with the—er, with the question why?"

I stared at him, puzzled.

"Do you mean that he will ask me to speculate on why anyone would have wanted to hurt me?"

"That has been, in effect, what he has been asking the rest of us to do for the past few hours. It has been very difficult to keep our own counsel, you will understand. That is why it might be better for you to delay seeing the gentleman until I have explained our stand to you. Of course, there is this. I did not want to ask you at once, but is it possible that you actually saw Mallick approach you?"

I had the sensation of one who has entered the room in the middle of a discussion. It was obvious that while I had lain unconscious, a great deal had been said between the others. Something in this displeased me. Were they assuming that simply because they had made certain decisions, I would abide by them?

"I saw a shadow, nothing more," I said evenly. "It could have been a man or a woman. I am in no way prepared to claim that it was Mallick."

An expression of disappointment momentarily wrinkled Mr. Harlow's bland face. "Well, of course a positive identification is not necessary," he said as though he were reassuring himself. "It is quite obvious to even the Chief Constable that he was the person responsible. Although, no doubt, I should not say so, it was a fortunate thing that he stumbled on the stairs. Justice has been served."

"How can you possibly be sure that Mallick was my attacker?" I demanded. My head was no longer aching, but I felt as though a tight band had been drawn about it. "Did someone see him?"

"No," Mr. Harlow said reluctantly. "However, it is quite simple to reconstruct what happened. He must have heard David coming up the stairs, and let me say that it is fortunate for you, my dear, that he did. As it

was, he must have dropped the cane and run for the
back stairs. They are very steep and narrow and it is
quite understandable that he might trip and fall,
particularly since he was not carrying a light."

I thought that he must have been referring to the
narrow stairs up which I had run that morning in my
flight from Jason. It was impossible to believe that that
had happened only twenty-four hours before. I seemed
to see Mallick's body lying sprawled in the dusty
corridor and shuddered. I had never liked or trusted
the man. Furthermore, if what Mr. Harlow said was
true, he had tried to kill me. And yet the thought that
he was dead appalled me. Violence would taint this
house forever.

"But why would he have attacked me?" I demanded.
"The man had no possible reason for wanting me
dead."

"Ah," Mr. Harlow said, drawing a deep breath.
"That was the question given considerable discussion
before the Chief Constable arrived. David alerted the
house as soon as he found Mallick's body, of course.
The boy who assists your grandfather was sent into
Oxford. If it had been a simple matter of a man falling
down a flight of stairs, of course, we might have waited
until morning. But since you had been attacked, it was
necessary to send for a doctor, and Mr. Bramwell
insisted that the police be informed, as well."

"By Mr. Bramwell, do you mean David or Jason?"

"Jason. And, of course, I quite understand his
insistence that the authorities be brought in. After all,
he is a stranger in this house. No doubt he was afraid
that some accusation might be leveled against him."

"I would have thought that might be true of all of
you," I said slowly. "Unless, of course, you are all able
to prove your whereabouts at the moment I was being
struck down."

As though suddenly aware that he was preventing

the heat of the fire from reaching me, Mr. Harlow muttered an excuse and moved closer to the bed.

"Has everyone such proof?" I insisted.

"As it happens, no," he conceded, "although I am sure the constable understands that that is quite beside the point. I was in my bedroom, as were the others. Even if it were not for his infirmity, your grandfather was clearly in no condition to have mounted the stairs, even though it was his cane which was used on you."

"But how could Mallick have gotten his cane?" I asked. "My grandfather was waving it about when I last saw him."

"Mallick assisted us in getting him to bed, the boy having fallen asleep on his cot in the dressing room adjoining his lordship's chamber. Mallick was the last to leave the old gentleman. It would have been quite possible for him to have taken the cane since your grandfather was in no—er, condition to notice such details. David, Mr. Bramwell and I went straight to our respective rooms."

"And yet it must have been some time later that David found me," I said, frowning.

"Yes. He has explained that, of course. He was concerned about his—your mother and decided to look in on her before retiring. It seems that it was of some concern to him that she insisted on keeping so many candles lit in her bedroom, particularly since she is inclined, I understand, to sleep deeply."

"But she was not sleeping," I protested. "When I was attacked I was just returning from her room. She was not there."

Mr. Harlow inclined his head. The dull, grey light of the gloomy morning struck his spectacles, making them opaque.

"Yes," he said. "Quite so. At my insistence that we all tell the truth—at least to one another—she admitted that she had gone to Mallick's room."

"But why?" I cried.

"It is this part of the story which makes it desirable for us to keep some little secrets from the police," Mr. Harlow said confidentially. "She explained, you see, that Mallick was in possession of the letters which were taken from your room."

Suddenly I felt exhausted.

"Go on," I said. "Why would Mallick have taken those letters?"

"You look quite pale, my dear," Mr. Harlow said hesitantly. "Perhaps I should continue my explanation at another time, after you have rested. Certainly you are not able to see the Chief Constable."

"Why are you so set on my not seeing him?" I said in a low voice. "Precisely what secrets are we supposed to be keeping?"

"Everything!" Mr. Harlow exclaimed with unusual energy. "Now that Mallick is dead many things have changed. It is not necessary for us to make our affairs public. Your mother has told the police that she was in her bedroom when you were attacked and it has been assumed that you were on your way to see her, rather than returning to your own room. These details make little difference to the police. Mallick struck you down thinking you were your mother, but since he is dead there is no need for the Chief Constable to know that. It would produce needless complications. We have all agreed on that."

I pushed myself higher on the pillows until my eyes met those of my solicitor.

"Unless you explain what really happened, I will insist on seeing the constable now," I said firmly. "You say that my mother claims that she went to see Mallick in his room last night because he had my letters. Go on from there, please, and be as concise as possible."

The note of command in my voice reminded me of my father. I was, apparently, destined to share his impatience with innuendo.

"Very well," Mr. Harlow said stiffly. "It seems that
we have misunderstood your mother's part in this
affair from the beginning. On the day the household
first received word of your father's illness, Mallick
came to her and announced that he was in possession
of important information."

My head had begun to throb again with a vengeance
and I fought the impulse to press my hands against it.
Suddenly life seemed like a kaleidoscope. The patterns
had shifted disconcertingly.

"That is, at any rate, what she told you," I
murmured.

"Unless we have reason to believe otherwise, I think
that we can accept her word," Mr. Harlow told me.
"Mallick, it seems, was brought up in this district. He
was, in fact, a nephew of Grace Evans and, as such,
privy to a good deal of information concerning her
relationship to your uncle. Shortly after Grace and her
father and the child left for Canada, Mallick went to
London where he was employed, first as footman and
then as butler in the households of various wealthy
families. Whether by plan or by accident he had
returned to the village where he was raised at about the
time your mother came to Ludden Hall. He applied for
the position of butler and was accepted. However, your
mother claims that she was unaware of his particular
background until he came to her offering information
damaging to your father."

I turned my head and pressed my cheek against the
blessed coolness of my pillow. I was in too much pain
to feel surprise.

"To be brief," Mr. Harlow went on, "he told your
mother not only about the secret marriage between
Grace Evans and your uncle and that there had been a
child, but he was also able to provide a Canadian
address. Nor did he stop there. He claimed that as a

child he had been witness to your uncle's murder by your father."

I clenched my hands in an attempt to fight off the pain which seemed to be tearing my head in two.

"Why had he kept silent for so long? How could she have believed him?"

"She wanted to believe," Mr. Harlow said. "She admits that to her own sorrow. She had kept her hatred and resentment of your father locked up inside her for too many years."

Did that, I wonder, explain her resort to laudanum? My mind was growing fuzzy.

"And so she wrote to Jason," Mr. Harlow went on. His voice seemed to have a sing-song quality as though he were luring me into sleep. I fought to stay awake. "And until yesterday she was willing to use Mallick as a witness to the—er, murder, if it was necessary. His motive in all this was what one might expect, of course. He demanded money in return for information, and your mother was so eager that she agreed, even though the amount demanded was beyond her private means. However, she assumed that Jason would be generous with her."

His voice drifted off and I became aware that I had closed my eyes. I opened them with an effort. I had to hear this all now.

"Go on," I murmured. "Do go on. Nothing you have said explains why he would have attacked me thinking I was she."

"Your mother claims that after she talked to you night before last she had second thoughts. She realized she was punishing no one but you. She doesn't hate you, child. In fact she says. . . ."

"I don't want to hear about her change of heart," I told him in a heavy voice.

"But it explains why she went to Mallick last night. She told him that there was to be no talk of murder, whether Jason could prove his claim to the estate or not. And Mallick told her it was too late for her to go back on her word. He waved a parcel of letters in front of her, letters he claimed to have taken from this room. He told her that they contained proof that your uncle was killed. Deliberately drowned. He said that your father had admitted as much to Grace Evans and that she made reference to the confession in her letters."

"He was lying," I whispered. "He must have been lying."

"We may never know that," Mr. Harlow said. "When your mother left his room she warned him that she would not be blackmailed. Presumably that was when he decided to kill her. Probably he came up the back stairs to wait for her. But she lingered downstairs in the sitting room, and it was you instead of her that he saw by her bedroom door. You know the rest."

"And the letters?" My own voice seemed to be coming to me from a great distance.

"I'm afraid, my dear, that they have disappeared. We searched the man's room thoroughly before the Chief Constable arrived. But the point is this."

He came to stand beside the bed and peered down at me myopically. He seemed to sway in the pale light.

"The police have been told that Mallick was a strange man, given to ungovernable behavior at times. We have, I think, successfully conveyed the impression that something you must have said to him provoked him to violence. Unreasoned violence. We must let the matter rest there, my dear. The man is dead. We must protect ourselves against any possible subsequent question that one of us was involved."

My sleep was deep and dreamless and I awoke to the thin watery sunlight of another day feeling curiously restored. Only the pressure of the bandage on my

forehead remained to remind me of the injury I had
suffered. My mind was clear and I remembered at once
everything that Mr. Harlow had told me as though it
were a story I had heard of a hundred times instead of
one heard once through a veil of pain.

A fire was burning briskly on the hearth but I
seemed to be alone. Sitting up, I flung the covers back
and saw a letter propped against a candlestick. With a
flare of relief I recognized Nelly's handwriting.

I tore the envelope open and scanned the brief
message. Her widowed sister in Glasgow was ill, she
wrote, and she had to go to her. She was, however,
uneasy about me and urged me to return to Sloan
Square as soon as possible. Following my orders as far
as she could, she had sent my trunk by rail. By the time
I received this it would be waiting at the Oxford
station. Her sister's address was penned boldly and
underlined. She hoped that I would write to her at once
and let her know what was going on. That was only
fair, she added, given that I had left her in "fair"
ignorance of what had happened. She ended by
repeating her wish that I return to London.

I sat holding the letter and smiling. How absurd of
me to have believed that anything had happened to
Nelly. Her obvious annoyance with me was only a
reassuring reminder of our old relationship and I
determined to write this morning and tell her that all
was well.

But then I remembered that my sense of well being
was based on shaky ground. I had survived a vicious
attack and Mallick was dead, but nothing else had
changed. It was still possible that my fortune would be
lost and with it not only Ludden Hall but the house at
Sloan Square. Nelly would scarcely find that
reassuring news, especially since she knew nothing of
Jason and his claim.

It occurred to me that perhaps in the hours I had

been asleep Mr. Harlow might have received some news concerning the matter of the inheritance. I was about to reach for the bell rope when the door opened and Rose appeared, carrying a tray.

Her delight at seeing me awake was so evident that I was cheered for a second time.

"But you must not get out of bed, Miss," she told me, flying about the room, plumping pillows and poking at the fire. "Not until the doctor comes, at any rate."

"Nonsense," I retorted, pulling on my dressing gown and addressing myself to tea and toast with relish. "Now, tell me what has happened."

"Well, Miss," Rose said, stationing herself at the side of the bed as though to keep me in it by force if necessary. "Everyone has been that concerned about you, although the doctor did say it was only rest you needed. The mistress would sit with you for hours and Mr. David, too, and when they were tired Mr. Jason came, although it seemed to me unfitting like, his not being a real member of the family."

Apparently the news of Jason's possible relationship to me had not filtered to the servant's hall. I found that I was strangely touched to think that so many people cared, and it was with a particular pang that I fancied my mother sitting by my bed. I realized that I need not hate her any longer, since, if what Mr. Harlow had told me was true, she had told Mallick that she could no longer countenance his willingness to bear witness against my father. She had caused trouble enough, to be sure, but I saw her now as someone to be pitied and perhaps someday loved.

Was that what my father had hoped for when he had sent me here? Had he realized all along that underneath the surface vulgarity, the weakness, even the selfishness there was something in her which could be stirred and stir in return?

I faced the fact that I would never know, and a fresh sense of loss overwhelmed me. If only he could be here now to clear up all the questions. All that I could do was keep my faith in him and believe, among other things, that if the fortune he had enjoyed and willed to me had not, in fact, been his, he had not known it. If I could only see those letters. The thought of them tormented me, obliterating all the well being I had felt a few moments before. I might have escaped the danger Mallick had represented, but he was not the only person in this house to wish me ill. Whoever had those letters was my enemy.

"Shall I go to tell your mother you're awake, Miss?" Rose asked tentatively. "She was dozing a bit when I last looked in on her, but she told me earlier that she wanted to know the minute you were yourself again. The others are at breakfast downstairs, but no doubt you'll want to see her first."

I stared at the Spode cup in my hand. I had to see my mother, of course. Thank her for the risk she had taken for my sake. Make amends. And yet I knew I would have to steel myself for the encounter.

I looked up, startled, as something struck the window nearest me, and Rose gave a little cry. We reached the casement together, and saw a strange sight. My grandfather, wrapped in a shawl and wearing his old top hat, sat in his Bath chair which had been wheeled to a point just below the window. Beside him the boy who was his attendant was just about to hurl another pebble.

Before Rose could stop me, I pushed the casement windows open and leaned out. The air was damp and fresh and a watery sunlight bathed the fading roses.

"What, ho, gel!" my grandfather crowed. "So you're yourself again, are you? Come down to see old Bertie. There's something I want to say. Will you come, gel?"

"Yes!" I cried, amused and curious. What a

character the old man was, grinning and brandishing his cane as he had been when I had first seen him.

His cane!

I caught my breath as Rose closed the window. Was that the same cane which Mallick had used to strike me down? Mr. Harlow had said that the butler had taken it from my grandfather's bedroom. Would they have returned it to him? More importantly, what did he want to say to me which required such an unusual approach?

"You aren't going down, Miss," Rose expostulated, backing toward the cabinet where my clothes were kept.

"Only for a minute," I told her firmly. "Is there any way I can get to the courtyard without the others seeing me?"

She hesitated and then sighed. How many times had I heard Nelly sigh in precisely the same way?

"There's stairs down to the courtyard from the dressing room adjoining, Miss," she said. "But you're not to go."

"Give me my fur-lined cape," I told her. "My grandfather may have something important to say to me. He can't come upstairs himself, as you know. And later they may try to keep me from seeing him alone. I won't stay in the courtyard for more than a minute, I promise."

"But if someone comes while you're gone, Miss. . . ."

"You can tell them that I'll see them in a few minutes," I told her firmly, opening the cabinet door myself and taking out the cape. "Tell them I'm dressing, if you like. Now, is this the door to the dressing room?"

Reluctantly she showed me the way. The dressing room had obviously not been used for many years. Dust clouded the air and the few furnishings had been pushed into one corner and covered with a cloth. The narrow stairway curved to the right and then abruptly to the left. Rose called something after me but I did not catch the words. At the bottom of the stairs there was a small door. I pushed it open and found myself face to face with my grandfather who had had himself pushed to the shelter of the building. Behind his chair the boy stood staring at me, wide-eyed.

"Dear Bertie!" I said, leaning down to kiss the withered cheek.

My grandfather beamed at me, disclosing a toothless lower jaw. There was color in his thin cheeks and he looked far less feeble than I had ever seen him. Perhaps, I thought, he relished the excitement of the past few days.

"Now you must tell me what it is you have to say at once," I warned him. "We can have a long talk later, but just for now no one but Rose must know I've left the room."

"Always liked a secret rendezvous," the old man chortled. "Pretty women like 'em, too."

I took one of his hands and held it tight, warming it.

"Tell me," I insisted. "Is it something to do with the letters? Do you know what's happened to the letters?"

His smile faded. "It's not the letters," he muttered, "it's the cane."

"This cane?"

I pointed to the gilt knobbed stick in his other hand.

"Gave it back to me, he did."

Oh dear, I thought. Is he going to ramble.

"Who gave it back to you?" I asked. "The Chief Constable?"

"That's who it was, gel. Didn't want to, mind you, but I said my piece. Can't get along without it, I told him."

"Is that what you wanted to tell me?" I said, trying to hide my disappointment. Perhaps it was true that he was turning senile.

"Don't play the fool, gel!" he admonished me. "I came to tell you not to believe them when they tell you Mallick stole it. They won't listen to me. Think I couldn't hold my drink. Think I don't know what was going on that night."

"The night they helped you to bed?" I asked him.

"Getting me out of the way before I said too much," he muttered. "Thought I couldn't see what was going on in my own bedroom."

"What *was* going on?" I demanded.

"Never you mind," he told me. "But you remember this, gel. The cane was gone before Mallick ever left the room. He was the last to go. The boy here knows, don't you, lad. They woke you up with all their fuss, didn't they. And you were there when Mallick left the room, weren't you?"

The boy nodded, gaping slightly.

"Is that true?" I asked him softly. "Didn't Mallick take the cane?"

"No, Miss," he said, stammering. "It wasn't in his hands when he left the room, I'll swear it. But one of the others must have taken it because when m'lord called for it, it was gone and that's the truth."

There was no time to put anything into perspective, although it had become dreadfully clear that I had to do so. For if Mallick had not taken the cane to use as a weapon, one of the others had. David. Jason. Mr. Harlow. There had been no reason for any one of them to have removed it from my grandfather's room under cover of helping him to bed unless...

But Rose was leaning from the window above, waving wildly. It took only a moment for me to hurry up the stairs and throw off my cape.

"It's your mother, Miss," Rose whispered, pulling down the covers of the bed. "She's outside in the corridor. Oh, but look at you with your hair all damp and tangled."

The expedition down to the courtyard had left me suddenly quite weak, and I let Rose arrange me against the pillows as though I were a child, let her brush my hair until it hung in smooth strands about my shoulders. Panting with exertion, she tucked the cape out of sight and ran to open the door.

My mother entered the room like a wraith. Her face was as grey as the dressing gown she wore and her eyes were so dull and lifeless that I knew she must have taken laudanum to prepare herself for this interview. Doubtlessly it had taken less courage to sit by my side while I lay sleeping than would be required to meet me face to face. I felt a pity for her which had nothing to do with scorn.

"Can you ever forgive me?" she began.

One glance from me was enough to send Rose scurrying from the room.

"There is no need to speak of forgiveness," I said in a low voice. "Here. Sit by me. You look quite ill."

My mother remained standing and her laughter had a wildness to it which startled me even more than her words had done. I felt a sense of utter helplessness. How was it possible that we could unravel the tangled strands of so many years?

"You are ill, not I," she said. Her voice was as heavy as her eyes, and yet both throbbed with something like excitement. "You could have been killed because of me."

"Do you believe then that Mallick intended to murder you?"

I could think of nothing else to say. Perhaps by speaking of the immediate past we could reconcile ourselves to the present, find our way to one another by some path which would have nothing to do with the humiliation of mutual forgiveness.

"That is what they say," she said wearily, dropping into the chair as though her legs, quite suddenly, would no longer support her. She bent forward until her hair covered her face. "That is what they tell me," she repeated.

"It was no fault of yours that I should have been outside your door," I said softly. "That he should have mistaken me for you."

There was a long silence.

"I have been a fool," she said, raising her head, brushing away the thick mass of auburn hair.

Our eyes met for a long moment, jolting my heart. Perhaps, in the end, all our words would be unnecessary.

"I must tell you everything," she said in a dull voice. Her long, white fingers went to her forehead.

"It's quite unnecessary," I began. "Mr. Harlow..."

"*I* must tell you," she insisted. "And yet it is so difficult to think."

"Later," I said soothingly. "Later you can tell me."

"I am addicted," she said. "The laudanum. I began so many years ago. To kill the pain. No, not a physical pain. I loved your father. I don't expect you to believe that. But it was true. And I loved you."

"Don't," I breathed. "Don't do this to yourself, I implore you."

She seemed not to hear me. Her eyes no longer focussed on mine, but seemed intent on something in the middle distance, something I knew that only she could see.

"I am a selfish woman," she said in a monotone as though reciting a litany. "All my life I have thought of no one but myself. And yet I have loved. You must believe me, Ruth. But it was always a selfish love. I wanted so much more than I could ever seem to give. Perhaps I could have been the wife your father wanted me to be. If I had tried. But it seemed easier—easier to indulge myself. All my life I have indulged myself. Even my hatred of your father was an indulgence. I could have admitted that he was right to send me away, to take you from me...."

"Perhaps," I said slowly, "he was selfish, too. He could have forgiven you."

I waited for the sense of betrayal which I knew should come. For the first time in my life I had made myself my father's judge. His jury. And found him wanting. Guilt would come like a coil of pain. And yet it did not. *It did not.* I took a deep breath and leaned back against the pillows, closing my eyes. Something vital to my being had changed. I would never be the same. I was aware of an overwhelming sense of relief.

I do not know how long we sat in silence, but when I opened my eyes she was smiling. It was as though I was seeing her for the first time. Perhaps, had we both been different women, I would have held out my arms, or she hers. But that was not necessary. We both knew it. We were, I realized, more alike than I had guessed.

"We will speak of the present then," she said. Some of the heaviness was gone from her voice. Reaching into the pocket of her dressing gown, she took out a bundle of letters and handed them to me.

"I went to Mallick that night to tell him he must give them to me," she said simply. "He refused. Later, when they found him dead, I went to his room. They were there, hidden underneath his mattress. I have not read them, Ruth. Not a word. They belong to you."

I took them from her and for a moment our hands touched.

"It all began with Mallick," she went on in a monotone, as though she were reciting a lesson which she had reviewed all too often. "I trusted him. It has been difficult to keep servants here. We are so—so isolated."

Her voice broke and I knew that she was thinking of

the years spent alone with a son who was not really her own and a father who must have been erratic company at best. For the first time I could pity her, but I could not find the words to tell her.

"When I heard that your father was ill and not expected to live, I mentioned it to Mallick. He was—he was someone to talk to."

I wished that she would not humble herself so. But perhaps it was necessary. Even more necessary was that I listen to her carefully. All had to be clear between us.

"How did you learn of my father's illness?" I asked her. "Did he write to you?"

"No, no. He never wrote. He even saw to the upkeep of the estate indirectly, through Mr. Harlow. The news came from him. When he was here to talk to the agent in July, he told me that your father's case was— hopeless."

How strange, I thought, that when I had asked Mr. Harlow to tell me something about my mother, he had managed to convey the impression that he had not seen her since she left London. Certainly I had had no idea that from time to time, over the years, he had come to Ludden Hall.

"But I meant to speak of Mallick," my mother said, rubbing her head. "When I told him about your father, he told me that there was something I should know. He had never mentioned his past life before, but he told me then that he had been a nephew of a Mr. Evans who had been estate agent here when your father and his brother were young men and their parents were still alive. I wish—I wish I had refused to listen to him. But I was curious. Your father had told me so little about his life before he met me. He was always secretive with me."

"And with me as well," I said in a low voice.

"Ah," she said and the word held a wealth of

meaning. Was she realizing, I wondered, that my
father's reticence had had nothing to do with his feeling
for her?

"Did your father never tell you of a Grace Evans
then?" she whispered.

"Never," I told her. "It was only when Jason came to
London that I discovered that my uncle had loved her,
had a child by her."

I held the letters close to my breast. Should I go on, I
wondered. Tell her that these messages had been
written by the very woman we were speaking of, that
they had been written not to my uncle but to the man
my mother had later married?

But she gave me no time to say anything. All of what
Mallick had told her came out in a rush as though it
was something of which she was trying to purge herself.
The tale of a marriage. A child. An inheritance which
had gone unjustly to the man she had married.

"And I believed him," she concluded sadly.
"Because I wanted to."

"Did you ask him why he had remained silent so
long?" I asked her.

"No," she said in a hard voice. "Oh, no. I was much
too eager to hurt your father. When Mallick said that
he had an address in Canada, I couldn't wait to write
the letter. I wanted—I wanted Jason to arrive before
your father died. I wanted to punish him. I wanted
revenge so badly. I think I must have been insane. I
didn't even think of what I was doing to you. And when
Mallick told me that he had seen your father murder
his own brother. . . ."

She broke off and I realized that she was weeping.

Moving to the side of the bed, I put one hand
tentatively on her shaking shoulders. And she did not
move away.

For what seemed a very long time neither of us
spoke. It had begun to rain again. Water ran down the

long windows like tears.

"You believed Mallick then," I said. "Do you believe him now?"

"I only know I don't want it to be true," she whispered, turning her pale face toward me. "I'm glad he's dead. Because he would have spoken out. Even when I told him that I wanted nothing said about that day when he was watching by the river . . . he wouldn't listen to me. It was the night he died. I went to him because he had told me about the letters. He said they would be his proof. I wanted them. I was going to destroy them. What happened in the past is past. Now that your father is dead. But once I had them I knew that you must be the one to decide."

The letters seemed to burn my hand, but I kept a tight hold of them. Whether they would be destroyed or not would have to be decided later. Now I had to know all that she could tell me. And there were two questions which had to be answered.

"Why did Mallick refuse to keep silent?" I asked her. "My father meant nothing to him."

"He wanted money," my mother said. She spoke so softly that I could scarcely hear her. "In the beginning I promised him money. He knew that unless the estate went to Jason there would be nothing for me. I told him that Jason wanted nothing said about how his father might have died. But Mallick insisted that he would make the story public unless the fortune changed hands. It all seems so confusing now. I only know that the night he died, I would have done anything to be rid of him."

"But why did you change?" I asked her. That was the second question. The most important question.

Her eyes met mine.

"Because I love you," she said slowly. "I tried to pretend that you meant nothing to me. That first day, after you left, I couldn't bear the pain of it. That was why I took so much laudanum. Perhaps I hoped that I would die. And then, later, when I was conscious again, I tried to play the role I had set for myself. I even thought of accusing you of having tried to poison me. I tell you I must have been insane. When you came back to Ludden Hall, when you came to me that night . . . oh, Ruth, I knew then that I couldn't go on. If hurting your father meant that I would hurt you so much. . . ."

I felt as though I could not breathe. She had called herself a fool, but I had been a fool as well. How could I have ever thought that I did not want her love?

"I've hurt so many people," she went on, her hands gripped tight together as though it were taking what remained of her strength to say the final words. "I could only think of myself. What I wanted. I tried to destroy you. And David . . . David."

"What has David to do with this?" I demanded.

"That night when I left Mallick's room I met him," she said in a low voice. "I must tell you this, Ruth. I must tell someone. Because, you see, he saw I was distraught. He asked me why and I tried to explain. But it was all a jumble of words. Now, thinking back I'm so afraid."

"He may have thought that somehow you were in league with Mallick to hurt me. I can't remember what I told him. Except that there were letters which must be destroyed. That they were yours. That Mallick had them now and would not give them up. He—he rushed away from me. I heard him on the stairs."

She did not have to say any more. Her agonized expression told me all I had to know. She was afraid that in a moment of passion, convinced that he must protect her, David had attacked me. Murdered Mallick.

"The cane," I began. "Was David carrying the cane?"

The eyes she turned on me were bewildered. Before

A HERITAGE OF STRANGERS 195

she could answer a knock came at the door. And then, although I made no response, it opened. Rose was standing there.

Burying her face in her hands, my mother rose and rushed past the girl, weeping wildly.

"Go with her," I told Rose. "See that she quiets herself in whatever way is necessary. But stay with her. There must not be another overdose. Do you understand me?"

"I understand," Rose said, flushing. "No need to worry, Miss. No harm will come to her."

Chapter Eleven

ONE PART OF my mind told me that I should be with my
mother now. But Rose was trustworthy. She could
administer a safe amount of laudanum if, as I
suspected, that would be necessary. As for me I was too
shaken by what my mother had told me to be of
immediate use to her. Could it be possible that David
in a fit of passion had murdered? I knew that he loved
his mother deeply. Time and time again in the short
while I had been here I had seen proof of it. I could even
believe that he might have killed Mallick to protect her.
But it was not possible that David could have struck
me down. I could not believe *that*.

And yet how could I trust my judgement now that it had been proved that I had so often been wrong in the past? Because my father had loved me I had been incapable of believing that he could be anything but just. Kind. Gentle. And, it followed, forgiving. But the man my mother had married had been many other things to her. Unwise. Thoughtless. Uncaring. And, in the end, bitterly unforgiving.

Leaning back against the pillows, I pressed the letters to my cheek. In a moment I had to read them. There could be no further delay. But before I did I had to acknowledge what I had so lately learned. Love must not be blind. Neither must it demand perfection in its object. I had been wrong to imagine that my father was without fault. It was a relief to me to realize that I could love him no matter what he had been or done. And my mother, too. Just as she would love David even if what she feared were true.

My fingers trembled as I untied the faded ribbon and unfolded the first letter. What I was about to read might bring me pain. I knew, from having briefly glanced at these pages when I had first found them, that Grace Evans had addressed my father as one might a lover. "My dearest Franklin." That was how the first began. And I knew that I was troubled deeply by the fear that I might discover that the child she had borne had not been fathered by my uncle. I could be strong. But if Jason were to be brother and not cousin, then my world would truly topple about me. I had to be honest enough to admit that.

The letters were written in a flowing hand. Grace Evans might have been only the daughter of an estate agent, but quite obviously she had been well educated. Each letter was carefully dated and I shuffled through them rapidly to see that they were in order. The first had been written on March 24th and despite the salutation it was not, as I had thought, a love letter but rather an apparent response to one.

"You are, as you must know, dear to me," she had written. "But as a brother. We have known one another since childhood and it is natural that we should feel affection, in spite of the differences in our stations. But please, my dear, do not pain me by writing again as you have. Next year you will be at Oxford—a young gentleman with a great future. The three years difference in our ages allows me a certain license. You will feel quite differently when you are at university with your mind completely occupied with important matters, and then you will thank me for these words of caution. Do not think that I fail to understand you when you speak of passion. Indeed I understand too well. But I will say no more except to assure you that I will always be your fondest friend."

I felt a great sense of relief. Then there had been no love affair between them. When she spoke of understanding passion, she must have been referring to her relationship with my father's brother. And if that were so, Jason's status as my cousin—if, indeed, he was any relation to me—was assured. Eagerly I turned to the next letter, this one written in May. It was obvious that since the last exchange they had met, probably during a school recess when my father would have returned to Ludden Hall.

"I know how painful it was to you to discover the truth," she began abruptly. "Your father and mother have been told now, and, as you can imagine, it was a great shock to them. Harry and I are to be married tomorrow in private at Ludden Hall. The child must have a father and although I should feel nothing but shame, I would be completely happy—as Harry claims to be—were it not for the fact that I have brought disaster to him. You will know more of this soon. Your father, in his wrath, has disinherited your brother. It is already an accomplished fact for he lost no time in calling his solicitor from London to change his will accordingly in your favor. Harry is to be given an adequate allowance on the condition that he and I go to Canada at once. No one here is to know of the child or even, if possible, about the marriage. Your father has set the terms. Even our marriage is to be kept secret. My family has been sworn to silence on the condition that if word of this becomes public knowledge, even the allowance will be withdrawn. If your father had had his way, I would have been sent abroad alone. But Harry insisted on the marriage. And so he has lost everything because of me. He claims not to care, but I can see the change in him. That alone mars my happiness. Perhaps, dear Franklin, if you were to return home no matter for how short a time, you could somehow help your brother to face the difficult days ahead. Until we leave the country he will remain at Ludden Hall as though nothing had changed. But I fear some sort of breakdown. He behaves so strangely...."

The remainder of the letter was lost to time, the violet ink faded to a shadow.

I felt breathless as though I had received a physical blow. This had to be true. She had written that a new will had been made. My uncle disinherited. And the solicitor called from London for that purpose could have been no other than Mr. Harlow's father. Yet, if this were true, why had I not been told? Why had Mr. Harlow pretended that if Jason could prove himself to be my uncle's legal son, he would be heir?

The answer might be in the next letter. I was almost afraid to read it. My father had taught me that the past existed to be re-examined. And yet I felt like an intruder in time. In an effort to wipe away this strange sense of guilt, I reminded myself that my father had deliberately left these letters to be discovered by me. No secret had been made of the gravity of his illness from the moment it had been discovered. He had known that he would die even when his health was still sound enough to allow him to spend long hours alone in his study. He could have destroyed the letters, but he had not.

But why had he simply left them to be found when he was gone? Why had he not told me the truth himself? Restlessly I rose from the bed and wrapped myself in my dressing gown. Rain was still dripping dolefully down the face of the long windows. The courtyard below was desolate. I stared down at it as though it could provide me with the answers to my questions.

If my father had wanted me to know of his past, he could have told me. If he had wished me to be reconciled to my mother he could have sent me to Ludden Hall while he was still alive. Had he believed me to be too impressionable? Yes, I could understand that. He had, after all, had reason to see my mother as an unfit influence for a child. He might have delayed purposely, knowing that the older I was when I was reunited with her, the more capable I would be of making a judgement which was not his but mine.

And that *had* happened. I was willing to forgive her as he had not been able to bring himself to do. In sending her the jewels and the letter he had released her from the threat of disgrace which had hung so long over her head. And, in sending me with them, he had indeed opened the door to reconciliation.

But why had he not told me that his brother had been disinherited, that the fortune had come to him second hand? Had it, perhaps, pained him too much even to discuss the matter? It must indeed have been a traumatic period in his life. He had loved Grace Evans with all the fury of adolescence. And he must have hated his brother for having brought her to disgrace. Perhaps a natural delicacy had made it impossible for him to speak of a child fathered out of wedlock.

The fire in the hearth had died to ashes, but it was not the chill which made me shiver. There was one last truth to be learned and I could not be certain that this last letter, which I held in my hand, would explain the circumstances of my uncle's death. Anything was better than not knowing. I went closer to the window and unfolded the last sheet.

"You must not blame yourself, my dear Franklin," it began. "There is no question in my mind that you tried to save him. It was clear to me that morning when Harry and I met in the garden that he was deeply troubled. It was not simply the loss of his fortune, for you know, as do I, that your brother was not a man who put great stock in worldly wealth. But it was a combination of two other factors which broke his mind and spirit. You know full well how dearly he loved Ludden Hall. I think that in the end he could not bear to leave it. And to have been cast off by his father was dreadful. To have stayed on in that house as a son and not a son... oh what a fool I was, dear Franklin, to think that the love Harry and I shared would be enough. I may seem to you to write these words calmly, but I am living in an agony of spirit which cannot be described. I think that were it not for the child I carry I would follow my beloved husband down that last dark path. But I write to you as one who must have the truth known. My cousin, young Mallick, witnessed what happened during those last dreadful moments when you tried to save Harry. But he is only a child and speaks irresponsibly of what he saw. That struggle in the water... oh, I cannot bear to think of it. But, for your protection, Franklin, if, after my father and I have left the country there would be rumors that you did not try to save Harry, I enclose this note which gives firm assurance of my husband's tragic intention. And now, dear brother, I must say goodbye. We leave for Southhampton tomorrow. Your own father, in his grief, has granted me the allowance which was to have been Harry's. I fully understand that my child, should he be a son, can never be the heir. I will start life in a new land. And you. You must learn to forget."

The note which had been enclosed had slipped to the floor. Crouching, I read it with eyes which would scarcely focus on the few brief lines.

"Forgive me, my darling Grace," my uncle had written. "I cannot think clearly, but it seems I cannot bring myself to live away from this house which I have loved for so long. All my identity exists here. It was my home and soon will never be again. I had a father and now I have him no longer. Had he died, had Ludden Hall burned to the ground, I could have faced the future. But there is only a dark void before me. And I must become a part of it. If this be madness then I only know it cannot be denied."

I found that I was weeping. Not only for the tragedy which lay so far in the past, but for the horror which must have remained as clear as crystal in my father's memory until the moment of his death.

I heard a sound and, looking up, saw the door to the bedroom opening. If there had been a knock, I had not heard it. Mr. Harlow's bespectacled eye took in the disarray of the bed, the trail of letters leading to where I sat, my head against the window seat.

"My dear child," he said softly, turning the key in the lock and pocketing it. "So at last you have learned the worst."

I stared up at the solicitor blankly. How could he
speak of the worst when I had learned only the best.
My father had been guiltless. He had neither murdered
his brother nor cheated him of his fortune. Jason was
not brother but cousin. Ludden Hall was mine. I
should have been beside myself with relief and joy, but
instead I was afraid.

I let Mr. Harlow help me rise from the floor. He
seated me on the window seat as carefully as though I
were a china doll, something to be easily broken.

"You look pale, my dear," he said gently. "Here, let
me open the window behind you. A bit of air ... are
you quite wrapped? Here let me put this blanket
around you. It's obvious that you have received a
shock. When your mother told me she had found the
letters and given them to you, I came at once. Poor
woman, she seemed quite distraught, but one of the
maids is caring for her. Quite a capable young woman.
I believe her name is Rose. I asked her to see that we
were undisturbed."

The length of his speech had given me time to put
my thoughts in order. The air through the open
window was flecked with rain, but I found its freshness
stimulating. So many questions had been answered in
so short a time. But there remained one more.

"Why did you pretend to take Jason's claim
seriously?" I asked the round faced man beside me.
"Your father must have told you that my uncle was
disinherited before Jason was born. You must have in
your possession the revised will leaving everything to
my father."

While I spoke Mr. Harlow engaged himself in
picking up the scattered letters. Even the ribbon was
retrieved but instead of wrapping it about them, the
solicitor began to shred them into small pieces. Slowly
and deliberately he tore each sheet into fragments and

scattered them on the floor.

The act was accomplished before I could make a move to stop him. Instead I cried out, at the same time pressing my hand against my mouth.

"Why did you do that?" I demanded.

"If you will only think, you will realize why," Mr. Harlow said slowly, coming to sit beside me and beginning to finger his watch chain in the old, familiar way.

He smiled at me benevolently, the way he had so often smiled before.

"Perhaps it will be less time consuming if I explain," he went on. "In spite of my directions to Rose, we might be disturbed. And I would like you to know the truth, my dear. Perhaps it is the last favor I can do for you."

"Why did you let me believe that I might lose my fortune?" I said in a low voice.

"It began with your father's pride in you," Mr. Harlow said quietly. "He was always a proud man. It explains his rejection of your mother. But that is beside the point, perhaps. You will remember, of course, the careful coaching which he gave you concerning his investments."

"Of course," I said. "I memorized them. I know the value of everything he owned."

"It was a pity that your father insisted on your being so well informed," Mr. Harlow said, smiling. "For many years he himself had not dabbled in such matters. It was only when he was dying that I realized you had been entrusted with a certain knowledge of his—shall we say, Value. I believe, in fact, that he requested that on his death you should review the matter of the investments with me in considerable detail."

"Yes," I said. "Why should I not have done so? I had a bent for mathematics which he did not share. He told me that I should keep a close eye on my assets."

"He said much the same thing to me," Mr. Harlow continued pleasantly. "It was shortly after he realized that his illness would be terminal. He explained that what little energy he had left should be expended on his book. The subject was Delphi, I believe."

"Yes," I murmured. "It was only natural that the hours left to him should be dedicated to his scholarship."

"That, of course, was his mistake," Mr. Harlow said blandly, taking off his spectacles and rubbing them with a spotless handkerchief. "It gave me time, you see, to make my plans."

"Plans?" I said. "I don't understand."

And yet I did. Somewhere in my mind the pieces of the puzzle had been put together and yet I cared not to look at the picture they created.

"My frequent visits to this house. . . ." Mr. Harlow began.

"If you have been coming here regularly over the years," I interrupted, "why did you let me think you had not seen my mother since she left Sloan Square?"

"A small deceit," he told me cheerfully. "And quite excusable, as you will see. As I said, my frequent visits to this house put me in touch with the unfortunate Mallick. I have always been a fair judge of men's characters and I saw in him one who was infinitely greedy. I expressed an interest in the past and discovered, at length, that he had been a witness to your uncle's drowning. Like any child his memory was—shall we say, malleable. He had, at the time, the impression of a struggle. It was a simple matter to convince him that he had seen, not an attempted rescue, but a successful murder."

"You!" I cried. "You convinced him of that?"

Mr. Harlow replaced the spectacles on his nose.

"It was not a difficult job, I assure you, my dear. Particularly since there was money in the offing. I made him see that your mother would willingly pay generously for her revenge on your father. And there was a certain amount to exchange hands between Mallick and me. A pittance, really, but to a man such as him, a fortune."

"But why?" I demanded. The air behind me was too chill. It penetrated the blanket, but I could not move. The scattered bits of Grace Evan's letters formed a barrier between me and the bed.

"I knew, of course, that your uncle—Jason's father—had been disinherited before your uncle's death," Mr. Harlow told me. "And I also knew that your father had never spoken to you of how he had happened to inherit. He once made it quite clear to me that the old scandal was taboo. Once he was dead, however, it was a simple enough matter to destroy the 'new' will."

"But why?" I insisted. "Why would you do such a thing?"

"To protect myself, my dear," Mr. Harlow said fondly. "I know that to people like you and your father, the favored few who do us the honor of managing their property, money is a vulgar matter. But to a poor working man like myself..."

"You robbed my father!" I exclaimed.

"How quick you are, my dear," Mr. Harlow said. "And how quickly after your father's funeral you would have insisted on examining the books. And discovered the truth. I anticipated all this many months ago when I learned that he was ill. I made my plans quite carefully."

Suddenly it was all clear to me.

"You gave Jason's address to Mallick," I said. "You were responsible for bringing him here to England."

"Actually, as you know, your mother wrote the letter," Mr. Harlow said. "But, yes, the address did come originally from me. It was an easy solution and I like to think a very clever one. With all evidence of the disinheritance destroyed and your father dead, there was nothing and no one to prevent Jason from inheriting. I knew your mother knew nothing of it. The only other person who might have been told was Nelly. At times, directly after your mother left him, your father confided in her, I believe. That was why I made certain she would not join us here directly."

"You—you sent her a bogus message from her sister?" I gasped.

"Quite so," Mr. Harlow said pleasantly. "No doubt the two women will enjoy a little visit with one another in spite of the hoax. Of course I cannot plan on having Nelly delay her return. However, matters will be settled quite satisfactorily before she can arrive here, I believe. As I said my plan involving Jason's inheritance was a clever one. He knows nothing of the amounts invested. The loss of a few thousand pounds will mean nothing to him. You are the only person who could have looked at the books and—well, made certain charges which would have greatly inconvenienced me."

I stared at him, alert now. Warned. Impervious to the cold wind blowing on my back.

"You embezzled...."

"A crude word, my dear, but, I fear, accurate. And yet those who know nothing of such matters will not suspect that any crime has been committed."

"I will tell Jason!" I cried. "I will tell him everything."

"But that would be my undoing, my dear," Mr. Harlow said gently.

He was leaning close to me now, his breath warm on my cheek.

"You can't prevent me from telling the truth," I whispered. "Take your hands off my arms."

"No, my dear," Mr. Harlow crooned. "I am afraid that it is in my best interest for those who next enter this room to find these scattered fragments of letters, letters which proved to you that your father was indeed a murderer. In your horror, what could be more natural than that you would seek to take your own life? The estate will, of course, revert to Jason. And he will ask no awkward questions, uncoached by you."

"I will not commit suicide," I declared. "What sort of fool are you? I would never take my own life."

"Then I will take it for you, my dear," Mr. Harlow murmured quietly, grasping my shoulders. "You should have died the other night had I aimed the cane more accurately. The plan was to have Mallick found dead and you as well. It was a great disappointment to me. But all will be well. Yes, that's right, my dear. Lean back. Lean back. The courtyard is just below. You will feel nothing."

I struck out at him as he pressed me backward. I struck at his face. His spectacles clattered to the floor. And still he continued to press me backward.

I struck at him again, and in that moment I heard the sound of pounding at the door.

"Help me!" I cried.

My words were lost in the sound of fists on the door. I tried to call again, but his hands were about my throat. His face beamed down at me. Below lay the courtyard. Nothing behind me now but air.

And then I heard the sound of splintering wood. There was a struggle. For a moment I thought that I was falling. And then I found myself being drawn into the room. Mr. Harlow's face had been replaced by Jason's.

*   *   *

There were, I realized, a good many people in the room. A man I did not recognize but who, on account of his uniform, I took to be the Chief Constable, was holding Mr. Harlow by the arm. The solicitor, lacking the spectacles I had struck from his nose, was looking about the room with an expression of vague bemusement. He made no effort to get away, and when David picked up his eyeglasses from the floor and handed them to him, he murmured his thanks as though someone at table had handed him the salt.

No one else spoke. My mother, her eyes dulled as though she were struggling against sleep, was standing in the doorway, and behind her I saw Rose wide-eyed, obviously excited. Jason, who had released me, stood looking about him like an actor who has forgotten his lines. Closer to me stood Professor Rankin with his black college gown thrown back over his shoulders like a cape.

It was the professor who broke the silence.

"Are you all right, Ruth?" he said and came and put his arms about me, holding me gently as my father would have done.

I hid my face against his shoulder and struggled to keep back tears of relief.

"David came to me this morning and told me everything," the professor said in a low voice. "About Mallick and his death. About the threat of your being disinherited. I couldn't understand that because I knew that the estate had come quite properly to your father. He never explained the circumstances, mind you. I told you he was reticent about his boyhood. But I did know that before his brother died, a new will was made out by your grandfather and that Franklin was heir. I never imagined that you did not know that, my dear, although I expect I should have guessed. After all, your father did not tell you so many things. But that is quite

beside the point now. When David said that Harlow
was here, I recognized the name and realized that his
father must have been the solicitor who administered
the estate when your father was in his minority. I knew
that the firm must be quite aware that there was no
question of the validity of your legacy. And that made
me very curious. Very curious indeed. At that point I
decided to interfere."

"The professor insisted that the police be told
everything," David said. Looking up, I saw him
bending over me. "We came back here at once,
although we never dreamed you might be in danger. If
we had delayed . . ."

My mother gave a faint cry and I saw that Rose was
now supporting her. By the time David reached the
door, she had gone quite limp. As though she were a
child, David gathered her in his arms and went off
down the corridor toward her room.

As though a signal had been struck, the Chief
Constable led Mr. Harlow from the room. The
solicitor offered no resistance, turning only to beam at
me as though, not five minutes before, his hands had
not been at my throat, as though he had never tried to
push me to my death.

"Something in his mind must have snapped,"
Professor Rankin said reflectively. Still holding me, he
reached out with one hand and closed the casement
window.

"She ought to be in bed," Jason said gruffly and
Rose, suddenly animated, literally flew into the room
and began to smooth the sheets.

"I'll see to the fire," Jason muttered, taking up the
poker.

There was something strangely awkward about him
as he went to the fireplace and I realized that he was the
victim of the same sense of shock I shared as I let the

professor lead me to the bed.

But I would not get into it, would not let Rose tuck the blankets about me. I had been frightened, but I was not a child. With one hand on the bedpost, I looked down at the shredded letters.

"They must be saved," I said and found that my voice was hoarse as though I had not spoken in a long time. "They prove that my father was—was an innocent man."

"Don't talk now," Jason said in a curt voice, poking at the coals. "You will weary yourself."

"Ruth must say what she likes," Professor Rankin said gently. "She must tell us everything if she wishes to."

"The letters were written by your mother," I said to Jason, "to my father. I can't expect you to believe me. Mr. Harlow has destroyed my grandfather's second will in order to save himself from a charge of embezzlement. These letters are the only proof. They must be put together."

"There must be a copy of the new will somewhere among your father's papers," the professor assured me. "I think there will be no difficulty. As for Mr. Bramwell believing you...."

"I would believe anything she told me," Jason muttered. The fire was blazing now and he stood away from it, his eyes on the floor. From the other side of the bed, Rose watched us, bewildered, her eyes going from face to face. No one suggested that she leave.

All I could really think of was what I had to tell Jason—that his mother had conceived him before her marriage, that because of it his father had lost his inheritance and, as a consequence, taken his own life.

"I—I can't give you so much pain," I said to him.

Jason raised his eyes and smiled ruefully.

"You could never hurt me by telling me the truth," he said in a low voice.

"I will make your task easier, Ruth," Professor Rankin said calmly. "Remember that the truth is always a catharsis—painful, perhaps, but bringing relief in its wake."

It was as though it were my father speaking. And so I told Jason everything his mother had written, clearly, with no elaboration.

"My father tried to save yours," I concluded. "There was nothing but love between them."

Slowly Jason came across the room until he stood before me.

"All of this is tragic," he said, "but you must believe me when I say it brings no pain, Ruth. I never knew my father, never dreamed of inheriting a fortune. My mother seemed a happy woman. She died, smiling, my hand in hers. I believe she had a good life. And the only fortune I want is the one I can create for myself. Will you believe me?"

My eyes lingered on his. The awkwardness between us had passed and I knew that it would not return again. He had spoken of his mother and I thought now of mine. David would care for her always, of that I was sure. And I would care, as well. There would always be enough love. When my father died, I believed he had left a gap which could never be filled. But that was not true. That was not the way he would have wanted it to be.

I realized suddenly that Professor Rankin had slipped out of the room. And so had Rose. Jason and I were alone together. He put out his arms and I moved forward. And in the moment of our first embrace I heard Nelly's voice in the hallway. At the same time there came another sound—familiar and as reassuring—the sound of pebbles striking the window.

"Later," I told Jason in a low voice. "Later we will be alone."

When Nelly came blustering into the bedroom, her

face scarlet, puffing slightly, Jason and I were standing by the window, waving at my grandfather below in the courtyard, top-hatted in his Bath chair and gesturing in a perfect frenzy of curiosity with his cane.

BERKLEY BESTSELLERS YOU WON'T WANT TO MISS!

CHILDREN OF DUNE   (03310-4—$1.95)
  by Frank Herbert

THE CHINESE BANDIT   (03403-8—$1.95)
  by Stephen Becker

DRY HUSTLE   (03661-8—$1.95)
  by Sarah Kernochan

ESTABLISHMENT OF   (03288-4—$1.95)
INNOCENCE
  by Harvey Aronson and
    Mike McGrady

FINDING MY FATHER   (03456-9—$1.95)
  by Rod McKuen

THE FIRST DEADLY SIN   (03424-0—$2.25)
  by Lawrence Sanders

THE HOUSE ON THE HILL   (03648-0—$1.95)
  by Jonathan Black

INDIGO NIGHTS   (03629-4—$1.95)
  by Olivia O'Neill

Send for a list of all our books in print.

These books are available at your local bookstore, or send price indicated plus 30¢ per copy to cover postage and handling to Berkley Publishing Corporation
390 Murray Hill Parkway
East Rutherford, New Jersey 07073

CHILLING GOTHICS FROM BERKLEY

MORE BESTSELLERS FROM BERKLEY

THE GHOST OF FLIGHT 401   (03553-0—$2.25)
  by John G. Fuller

THE KINCAIDS   (03442-9—$1.95)
  by Matthew Braun

MOSCOW FAREWELL   (03385-6—$1.95)
  by George Feifer

ONCE AN EAGLE   (03330-9—$2.75)
  by Anton Myrer

THE ONCE AND FUTURE KING   (03174-8—$2.25)
  by T.H. White

THE TALISMAN   (03492-5—$1.95)
  by John Godey

THE TANGENT OBJECTIVE   (03441-0—$1.95)
  by Lawrence Sanders

THE YANKEE AND   (03493-3—$1.95)
COWBOY WAR
  by Carl Oglesby

Send for a list of all our books in print.

These books are available at your local bookstore, or send
price indicated plus 30¢ per copy to cover postage and
handling to Berkley Publishing Corporation
390 Murray Hill Parkway
East Rutherford, New Jersey 07073